NIGHT OF THE PROM

"Romance," Barbara grumbled. "Isn't there enough romance in 'Love Blossoms Eternally,' that silly prom theme they came up with?"

"Hey, what's wrong with that?" Michael said.

"It's stupid, that's what's wrong," Barbara argued. Inside she knew there really was nothing wrong with the theme or with romance for that matter. It was a case of putting down something she never could have.

"Well, I kind of like the idea of a bunch of seniors dancing around, celebrating our escape from this institution. What if I demonstrate?" In a flash Michael jumped to the floor and spontaneously spun Barbara in circles around the cramped room.

It happened so quickly Barbara could only go along with Michael, but she felt a strange sensation that she couldn't quite place. She realized with a start that it was one of the few times she'd been held so close by a boy, and the feeling was not at all unpleasant. But she couldn't let Michael know that . . .

Bantam Sweet Dreams Romances
Ask your bookseller for the books you have missed

Night of the Prom

Debra Spector

BANTAM BOOKS
TORONTO · NEW YORK · LONDON · SYDNEY

RL 6, IL age 11 and up

NIGHT OF THE PROM
A Bantam Book/April 1982

Cover photo by Pat Hill.

ISBN 0-553-20788-1

Published simultaneously in the United States and Canada

PRINTED IN THE UNITED STATES OF AMERICA

0 9 8 7 6 5 4 3 2

Night of the Prom

Chapter 1

"You can't have it!" Michael McNally said.

"I need the room, and I'm gonna take it," John Rush yelled back at the top of his lungs.

Barbara Vreeland listened to the clamor in the back of the room and sighed. Another typical day at the *Call*, she thought as she raised the volume on her radio a little to drown out the noise. It seemed to her that every month, almost on schedule, someone on the staff of the school paper got into some sort of argument. This month it was the sports editor and features editor. Barbara hoped they'd stop soon; as editor in chief of the *Call*, she would have to step in and referee, a chore she would prefer to avoid. "Not today," she muttered under her breath, brushing a glob of rubber cement onto the clean white page in front of her.

"What did you say?" Her best friend, Kris, was standing beside the gray metal table that served as Barbara's desk.

1

"Oh, nothing," Barbara said, pushing back her long brown hair behind her ears. "Just reacting to the boys. I'll let them solve their own problems for a change."

"That'll be a first," Kris said, dropping her large pink nylon satchel on Barbara's desk. "Got a minute?" she asked, not waiting to see if Barbara did or not. "I've got great news." She paused before adding, "I'm in love."

"Who now?" Barbara asked, putting the rubber cement brush back into its container. She was always interested in hearing about Kris's "loves" and also was glad to take a break from the paste up.

"His name is Rob, he's new at the school—absolutely gorgeous—and he asked me out for Friday. I sort of 'accidentally' bumped into him on the cafeteria line and ended up spending the whole lunch period with him!"

Kris then gave Barbara a blow-by-blow description of the entire conversation. Although Barbara felt happy for her friend, she couldn't help envying her a little. Kris was able to pick up boys without even trying, while Barbara could count the number of dates she'd had in her four years at Clear Lake High on the fingers of one and a half hands.

"And you should have seen the girls at the P.K. table. They couldn't take their eyes off me," Kris whispered conspiratorially. "I think they were jealous."

2

P.K. was short for "popular kids," the girls who belonged to the three sororities at school. They hung around only with each other and dated the boys who belonged to the two school fraternities. Of course, if a boy were really special, they could overlook the fact that he wasn't a fraternity member. Barbara and Kris and the girls they hung around with considered the P.K.'s snobby.

"They don't have enough boys to keep them occupied?" Barbara wondered.

"You know those creeps—they've got to have every living person of the male persuasion running after them, or they feel inadequate."

"Wish I could have been there."

"They're not going to get their hands on this one—not if I can help it," Kris declared. Fishing through her bag, she came up with a half-opened pack of bubble gum. "Want some?" she asked Barbara as she popped a piece in her mouth.

"No, thanks," Barbara answered. She hoped for Kris's sake that Rob would last a little longer than her last boyfriends. Kris had been in love three times since September. Each "love" had ended abruptly after one date, and each time Kris had made a tearful vow that she would "never fall in love again." Until the next boy came along, Barbara always wanted to add.

"What do you have for me?" Kris asked. Barbara handed her some galleys, and Kris took a seat next to the side counter and began to paste up a page.

Meanwhile, Michael and John had raised their voices a couple of decibels louder, and the noise was becoming intolerable. Miss Gregg, the *Call*'s faculty adviser, hadn't arrived yet, and with no one else of authority around, Barbara could see she'd have to step in and settle the dispute after all. Turning around in her chair, she looked at them with her hardest "I'm the boss" look, but they hardly noticed. John, using the weight of his fullback-sized body, was pounding on the back counter, driving home his point. Michael was sitting on the ledge by the window, occasionally pointing his finger at John and trying to reason with him. He should know better than that, Barbara thought, bemused. Everyone knew you didn't use reason with John.

Her arms folded, Barbara walked over to them. "What's the problem, guys?"

John stood up. At six feet, five inches, he was a full foot taller than Barbara, and he tried to use that height advantage to intimidate her. "*He* is the problem," he announced, pointing to the curly-haired features editor. "Do something about it."

Michael flashed an innocent-looking smile at Barbara. "All I want is room for my features. Room he's trying to steal."

"I need it, Barbara," John pleaded. "See?"

He flung a stack of galleys in front of her eyes, so close that it was impossible for her to focus. Pushing them back she saw they contained the copy of John's pet article on the history of the Clear Lake Stallion's basketball team.

"Barbara, would you tell him that nobody's interested in that stuff. It doesn't even deserve space on the sports page."

"Tell pretty boy over there he's wrong. I worked two whole weeks on this piece."

Barbara took her time answering. One of Clear Lake's star athletes, John had been named sports editor only because no one else wanted the job. He knew as little about journalism as Barbara knew about zone defenses, and she had to rewrite practically everything he wrote—including this article about the basketball team, which she found incredibly boring. She didn't think anyone besides Mr. Greene, the basketball coach, would care who had scored the most points in the 1957 championship game, but for some reason the article was so important to John that he'd threatened to resign if she didn't run it.

As bad as he was, she couldn't afford to lose him now. "I like your article," she said at last, hoping he wouldn't see through the lie. "But you've got to cut it to fit on the sports page."

"I can't do that."

"You have to," Barbara insisted. "You've got nine columns to work with, and you've got ten and a half columns' worth of copy. Something's got to give."

"Okay," he said, brightening, "what if I cut out one of the other articles?"

"I can't let you do that, or my head—and maybe yours—will be on the block." Last month she had made the mistake of yanking the wrestling article out at the last minute to make room for the upcoming swimming season schedule. She didn't think too many people would mind not reading about a bunch of guys rolling around on the floor with each other, but Mr. Putnam, the wrestling coach, had been furious. His team had just upset the previous year's state champions—and it was the first good news about the team in years. She wasn't going to make the same mistake twice.

"It's not fair," John said, tugging at the sleeves of his Los Angeles Rams T-shirt.

He acts like such a baby sometimes, Barbara thought. "Cut it," she repeated, "or I'll do it for you. And you know how much I know about sports." She looked him straight in the eye and gave him her best Cheshire-cat grin.

Barbara glanced over at Miss Gregg, who had come in just as Barbara's mediation effort had begun. She felt good about the way she had handled her temperamental sports editor but didn't think it would hurt to be given a vote of confidence by the young English teacher.

Smiling, Miss Gregg nodded silently, then sat down in her seat near the front and began to grade papers. The blond teacher had no qualms about the way Barbara was running the paper and saw no reason to interfere. She remembered all too well how her own faculty adviser had tried to run the whole show—and how she had resented it—when she had edited her own school newspaper only six years before. In fact, she couldn't help but notice how much Barbara reminded her of herself at that age.

"Yeah, cut it, John," piped Bobby, the *Call*'s assistant editor, who felt brave enough to speak up now that the issue had been decided.

"I don't have to listen to you." John sneered at the pint-sized Bobby, who came up to his armpits.

"But you'll listen to Barbara, right?" asked Michael.

"Okay, I know when I'm outnumbered," John said, sulking. He retreated to his seat against the back wall, where, in frustration, he took out a blue rubber ball from his pants pocket and began to bounce it against the Van Halen calendar on the wall.

"Thank you, Michael," she said, turning her attention to the features editor.

"Only trying to help," he responded. "I hate when people try to take over my pages."

"I thought I was the one who came to your assistance," she noted.

"You saved my life."

"I'd like to see page three in ten minutes," she said, getting back to business.

"Yes, ma'am," he said, retreating to his seat by the window. He gave John, who was still playing with the ball, an annoyed glance, then began sorting out the galleys that were balanced precariously on his lap.

Barbara returned to her layout of the front page, trying to block out the noise coming from the back of the room. I'm not going to let him get to me, she told herself as she pasted the banner on the top of the page.

"Here are the headlines," Bobby said, handing her a galley full of lines set in various type sizes.

"Thanks, Bobby." Bobby was a junior, and the likely candidate to replace Barbara as editor next year, As such, he hung on every word that came out of her mouth. Barbara had trouble adjusting to that kind of attention—it was as if she had a human puppy dog by her side all the time. Bobby's shaggy red hair and high, squeaky voice did little to dispel that notion.

"I hope you like them," he said, still standing over her shoulder.

"They're fine," she said.

"I kind of like this one," he said, pointing to a lead for the student council meeting. "It really says it all, don't you think?"

"It's only a headline," Barbara answered.

"What about this one? Do you think it works?"

"I said they're fine," she answered, getting impatient with him.

"But it's so important that they be right," he insisted. "Now take this one—"

"Does this meet with your approval, Madame Editor?" Michael, seeing Barbara's discomfort, had rushed right over with his neat, though hastily pasted, page three.

"Let me look," she said gratefully. Turning to Bobby, she motioned for him to leave.

As she glanced over the page containing the gossip column and profiles of outstanding students, Michael stood over her other shoulder, watching. "You could thank me for rescuing you from Bobby," he whispered.

"Thank you," she said obligingly.

"It's the least I could do to pay you back for before."

"I didn't do that for you," she said. "You just happened to have been right for a change."

He looked at her disapprovingly. "You're not going to win a lot of friends with that kind of attitude."

"Huh?" She looked up.

"That wasn't exactly the nicest thing I've heard all day."

"I didn't mean to sound unfriendly."

"Could have fooled me."

"Look, it's not easy being editor, especially when I have to deal with certain hotheads," she said in a low voice, motioning in John's direction.

Michael laughed. "We can't all be as easygoing and hardworking as I am."

9

"Or as conceited."

"Okay, I exaggerated," he said. "But you have to admit I do know what the public is interested in reading."

He has to rub it in, Barbara thought, remembering their big argument the month before. Needing room for the student council roundup, Barbara had wanted to cut the space allotted to the gossip column. She'd always secretly disliked the column. Besides the fact that it was being devoted almost entirely to the P.K.'s, it also reminded her of the parties and fun times she was missing out on. Michael had argued vehemently, however, that to cut it would be to deprive the school of the information they wanted to read. It was only after he came back with a petition signed by over two hundred students that she relented, but the episode still irked her. It almost hurt to be wrong.

"Listen, I've got an idea," he said.

"Nooo . . ."

"Barbara . . ."

"I'm sorry, go ahead," she said.

"We're starting that life management project next week, right? I thought it'd be a great topic for a feature."

"You mean a piece on what it's like to pretend to be married?"

"Something like that. What do you think?"

"I think I've got to admit that every once in a while you come up with a good idea. We'll schedule it for April." She looked at him as if to say, "You win this round."

"Thanks, Madame Editor."

"Do me a favor and cut out this Madame Editor stuff. My name's Barbara, in case you forgot."

"Anything you say there—Felix." He winked playfully.

Barbara glared at him for a second but decided it wasn't worth the bother. Michael McNally had always been trying to get the best of her—ever since they had had their first fist-fight in kindergarten. The name Felix went back to eighth grade when they had been paired together on a science project. She had had to have everything in its place before starting their experiments, while he preferred what he called "organized chaos." She had called it plain sloppy and had taken to calling him Oscar, from the TV show *The Odd Couple*. Naturally, he soon began calling her Felix, even though she was a girl. He still used the name whenever he wanted to tease her.

She wasn't sure why Michael was hassling her today, but she didn't have time to dwell on it. Barbara had the reputation of being a work-horse—a trait that didn't exactly guarantee in-stant popularity with Clear Lake's boys—but she didn't care to change. She loved working on the *Call* and took pride in the way she was able to keep up the quality of the newspaper. She even loved this office, with its walls full of old clippings and musty, old green-and-white school pennants. It was a home away from home for her, and the few touches she had added to the place—the posters on the back wall and the radio on her desk—helped make the place a little more comfortable.

A few minutes later Kris approached her with the page she was working on. "Listen, Barb," she said, popping another piece of gum in her mouth. "Don't let those guys get to you. You know boys."

"Yeah," Barbara said quietly, though both she and Kris knew she wouldn't win any prizes for being an expert on the subject.

"By the way, Kris, are they really going to hold the senior prom at the country club?" She was referring to the front page article Kris had written about the prom committee.

"Yep, they're making the final decision later this week."

"Why there?" she asked. "It's the most expensive place in town."

"Money doesn't seem to be a problem for the kids on the committee," Kris noted, shrugging her shoulders.

"But what about the rest of the seniors?" Barbara asked, her voice rising. "Everybody should have a chance to go to the prom, not just the rich kids. Wouldn't it be cheaper to have it someplace else?" If there was anything in the world she hated, it was the way some kids tried to leave out others. She didn't like the idea of the prom being too expensive for most of the class to attend.

"The gym is one of the other choices," Kris said, wiping the remnants of a burst gum bubble off her lips. "But it wouldn't be as romantic."

"Romance," Barbara grumbled. "Isn't there enough romance in Love Blossoms Eternally, that ridiculous prom theme they came up with?"

"Hey, what's wrong with that?" Michael spoke up. As a member of the prom committee, he had helped select the theme.

"It's stupid, that's what's wrong," Barbara argued. Inside she knew there really was nothing wrong with the theme—or with romance for that matter. She was putting down something she felt she'd never have. Turning to Michael she added, with a touch of sarcasm, "It figures *you* were in on it."

"It figures you would say something dumb like that. And you still haven't answered my question. What's wrong with the prom theme?"

"I can see it now," she said, rising from her seat and walking around to the front of the desk. "A big room filled with hearts and frilly decorations all illustrating the glories of everlasting romantic love. Sounds sickening to me." She folded her arms in front of her, her hands disappearing behind the folds of her long-sleeved shirt.

"Well, I like it."

"That figures."

"I suppose the idea of a bunch of seniors dancing around, celebrating our escape from this institution doesn't appeal to you, either," he said, eyes flashing.

"Why does it all have to center around romance?" she asked stubbornly.

"Because it's fun. Don't you think the idea of getting dressed up for one night and dancing to great music with your friends is fun? Didn't you have a good time at the junior prom?"

"I didn't go," Barbara said quietly, remembering the hurt she'd felt at not being invited.

"Oh," Michael said, surprised. "So you don't even know what I'm talking about. Here, let me demonstrate." In a flash he jumped up, grabbed Barbara, and cheerfully spun her in circles around the cramped room.

It happened so quickly Barbara could only go along with Michael as he led her through the waltzlike steps. She felt a strange sensation that she couldn't quite place as he held her close and danced her around the desk and toward the window. She suddenly realized that this was one of the few times she had been held so close by a boy, and it felt good. She wasn't about to let Michael know that, though.

"Okay, I get your point," she said, breaking away from his hold and catching her breath.

She could tell from the surprised expression on his face that Michael, too, had felt something happen. She half expected him to come back at her with something sarcastic, but he just stood there, a strange and confused look on his face.

She had to say something. "See, Michael, you're wrong. I like to have fun just as much as everybody else."

"So why are you so down on the prom?" he said, his voice subdued.

"I'm not against the prom. If you'd been listening, you'd have realized that my big gripe is that I don't approve of holding it at the country club. I'd rather see it someplace where more of the class could afford to attend."

"Nobody's made the final decision yet," Michael noted. "So why don't you do something about it?"

"I'll write an editorial." Barbara's dark eyes glistened with inspiration.

"Editorial," Michael scoffed. "A lot of good that'll do."

"What do you mean?"

"For one thing, the prom meeting's on Friday, and the paper won't be out till next week, so whatever you say will be too late. But even if you had the time, I don't think it would make any difference."

"A lot you know," she shot back. "Editorials happen to be one of the most powerful tools of the press."

"If anyone takes them seriously," he noted. He turned to the table beside him and picked up a copy of the previous month's issue. "Take this one," he said, pointing to the top of page two. 'Club Pledging: Is It Fair?' You think all you have to do is publish a bunch of words and that'll change everything?"

"I never said I guaranteed change."

"Well, do you know what the reaction to this little editorial was? The frats and sororities had a good laugh—and as far as I know, the rest of the school yawned away." He tossed the paper on the floor.

"Michael—" she sputtered, reaching down to pick up the paper. She was using all her energy to push back the tears that were brimming behind her eyes. His comments had stung her deeply. She took her editorials seriously, and she didn't like the idea of being laughed at behind her back.

"Hey, I'm really sorry," Michael said softly. "I'm sorry if I said something you didn't want to hear, but I think I owe it to you to tell you the truth. I don't think one of your editorials is going to change anyone's mind. But that doesn't mean I don't think you should do something."

"What do you recommend, joining the committee?" she shot back.

"Sounds pretty sensible to me."

Barbara looked at him, shaking her head in confusion. "You really think that'll do any good?"

Michael paused. He truly felt bad about knocking her editorials and hadn't meant to hurt her. "I mean it," he said. "Go to the committee and tell them what you think. It's your right as a senior to do it."

"I don't know."

"Think about it. I'll be there to back you up, too, though I doubt you'll need me."

"You will?"

"You happen to be right about the country club."

"I'll think about it," she said, surprised to see that Michael agreed with her.

"Good," he said smiling. "And, Barbara, one last thing?"

"Yes."

"Save a dance at the prom for me."

Chapter 2

It was close to five-thirty by the time Barbara left the *Call*'s office with Kris. Dusk had already turned the sky a grayish blue, and a few stars were finding their way into the midwinter sky. It was unusually cold out for this part of southern California, and Barbara found herself hugging the ends of her gray cotton jacket close as she hurried to her car in the school's parking lot.

Barbara was thrilled with the new-to-her car, a shiny VW Rabbit, whose brown exterior perfectly matched the color of her eyes. It had been a sixteenth birthday present from her parents, and she took care of it well, even to the point of learning how to change the oil. She liked to do as much as she could herself, which was something that Kris, for one, could never understand.

"It's cold in here." Kris patted the arms of her tan corduroy blazer. "Did you put the air conditioner on by mistake?"

"No." Barbara fiddled with the controls, but

cold air continued to pour out of the vents. She revved the engine to see if that made a difference. It didn't.

"I'll just have to suffer." Kris pretended to pout.

"It's only a ten-minute ride," Barbara pointed out. "Be brave." She shifted the car into reverse and pulled out of the parking lot.

"Are you really going to join the committee?" Kris asked a few minutes later when they had stopped at a traffic light.

"The prom committee?" It was a question she had been thinking about ever since Michael had suggested it.

"What else?" Kris answered.

"Why do you want to know?"

"Aren't you being the sensitive one. I was just curious."

"Oh." Barbara stared ahead at the road.

"I happen to think it's a marvelous idea," Kris continued.

"What makes you think so?"

Kris smiled. "I can see it now. You trying to crusade against the P.K.'s. We could sell more tickets to that than to the prom."

Barbara didn't want to admit it, but she agreed totally with Kris. "You know," she said after a while, "I think I just might pop into the next meeting. When did you say it was?"

"Day after tomorrow. Oooh, won't Michael be surprised," Kris gently teased.

20

"Michael has nothing to do with it," Barbara said a little too hastily. At that moment she turned onto the tree-lined street where she and Kris had lived all their lives.

"Oh, no?" Kris asked mischievously. "Seems to me it was his idea in the first place."

"So once in a while he comes up with something that makes sense."

"I think there's more to it than that."

"What are you talking about?"

"Maybe he's got another reason for wanting you on the committee."

"Like what?" Barbara challenged.

"Come on, Barb, didn't you see the way he was looking at you today? I think he's got the hots for you."

Barbara nearly jammed her foot on the brakes. "You've got rocks in your head, Kris."

"Well you've got your head in the sand if you tell me you didn't notice anything different."

"Then call me Barbara Ostrich," she retorted. "He was only playing around as usual."

"You think that remark about dancing at the prom with you was a joke, too?"

"He was only being polite. Besides, he's got every gorgeous girl in school running after him. Why would he want to bother with plain little old me?"

Kris eyed her friend carefully. "Who are you kidding—'plain little old me,'" she mimicked.

"We both know that underneath that serious exterior lies the heart of a passionate woman, a woman ready for romance."

Barbara laughed. "I swear I don't know why I hang around with you sometimes." She shook her head.

"Because I'm the only one around who'll tell you what you need to hear."

"And what makes you such an authority?"

"I've known you longer than anybody—except your parents. And they don't count."

"That's for sure," Barbara said, a trace of resentment in her voice.

"But even I don't know everything about you. Face it, you're a mystery girl. I bet you intrigue him."

"You know this for a fact?" Barbara asked.

"Aha," Kris cried, raising her eyebrows. "I knew you were interested. No, I don't know what he thinks. But it kind of makes sense, doesn't it?"

"You airhead." Barbara laughed. "I'd have to be the last girl left on earth before Michael would ask me out. I'm not his type."

"And who is?"

She shrugged her shoulders.

"So how do you know it can't be you?"

"Because we've been mutual enemies since kindergarten."

"Haven't you heard of the expression 'opposites attract'?"

"What does that have to do with Michael and me?" Barbara asked.

Kris shook her blond hair. "You're pretty smart up here," she said, pointing to her head. "But when it comes to boys, you're about as intelligent as a mule. I bet if you peek under that layer of contempt you pretend to have for Michael, you'll discover a lot of things you like."

"And what if I do?"

"It'll be a match made in heaven."

"You're too much of a romantic. Real life doesn't work out that simply."

"I think you don't know how real life works."

"Oh, yeah?"

"How could you? You spend too much time reading stuff like this," Kris said, picking up Barbara's economics textbook.

"Something you ought to do yourself," Barbara said, trying to change the subject, which was starting to make her uncomfortable. "Mr. Rozzo is giving us a test on Friday."

"So I'll cram with you tomorrow night," Kris answered nonchalantly as Barbara pulled into the driveway that separated their families' stately Spanish-style houses. "I'll call you later, okay?"

"Won't have time. Got a physics test tomorrow."

"You *are* studying too much," Kris said, getting out of the car. Holding the door open a crack, she added, "Maybe I shouldn't be so critical. Michael may like brainy girls." With that she slammed the door.

Barbara thought about Kris's remarks as she went up the flagstone walk to the front door. Up to now she had felt she couldn't afford to think too much about boys, but she secretly hoped that some day a special boy would notice her. Was Michael the one she was waiting for? No, she told herself as she carried her books up to her second floor bedroom. A guy as carefree as Michael and a girl like herself would never make it together. Not in real life anyway. . . .

Chapter 3

Barbara's bedroom was a corner room with a window seat that looked out into the yard separating her house from Kris's. Barbara had always loved this room, with its antique white furniture and airy, spacious feeling. When she was little, she had spent hours sitting on the window seat, holding one of her yarn dolls and daydreaming about faraway places. It was easy to do then, in the days when the room was wallpapered with fairy-tale heroes. Over the past several years Barbara had spent a lot of time tailoring the room to fit her newer likes. Gone was the wallpaper, replaced by several coats of light blue paint. One wall was completely covered with cork, and she had put up posters of Tom Petty and Bruce Springsteen, the issue of the first *Call* she edited, a Clear Lake button, and a few snapshots of her with her friends taken at the beach the summer before. The frilly white bedspread and gauzy canopy she'd had as a child had been replaced by a blue and white patchwork quilt, which went well with the room's dark blue carpeting. Only the furniture remained the same. That, plus one yarn doll, which Barbara kept on the window seat for sentimental reasons. At this moment it was sharing the spot with Macbeth, her frisky cocker spaniel.

She had had dinner, and was sitting at her desk, her pen keeping time with a song on the radio. She had it turned up loud, the way she liked it. Her notebook lay open in front of her.

Her concentration was broken by a knock on her door. Quickly she hid her notebook under the physics text, which she opened hastily and placed right under her reading lamp.

"May I come in?" Her father poked his head through the door.

"Sure, Dad," she answered, turning to face him. Macbeth jumped off the window seat and, tail wagging, went to greet Barbara's father.

A tall, hearty man in his early fifties, he strode purposefully into the room. The flecks of gray in his otherwise dark hair gave him a distinguished look that seemed quite appropriate for the editor of Clear Lake's weekly newspaper.

"How many times do I have to tell you—you can't learn anything with that junk blaring in your ears." He turned the radio off.

"Oh, Daddy," she challenged. "I do just fine. And I like studying with music on."

He glanced at the open physics book. "I thought you already had covered the basics of velocity."

Barbara saw she had opened the book to the second chapter. "Oh, yeah, we did. I'm just reviewing it. We're having a test tomorrow.

"Good girl," he said, pleased with her answer. "Remember, you must keep on the right track—you could really mess up if you don't concentrate."

Barbara sat there waiting for a speech about the perils of a wasted life—something she wasn't too familiar with yet. As it was, she didn't even get much of a chance to challenge the strict curfews her father imposed.

"Something bothering you? You look troubled."

"It's nothing. Just tired from studying," she said, not wanting to tell her father she had been wishing that they could have a nice talk with each other just once—instead of always going on about homework and grades.

"Well, keep up the good work. I want to see an A on that physics test," he said. "They don't like sluggards at Stanford."

"I haven't been accepted there yet," she noted.

"You will. It's what we've been working toward all these years," he said with certainty, the faintest of smiles beginning to cross his lips.

"I'm not so sure I want to go there anyway," she said casually.

"Nonsense. It's one of the best schools in the country. You're going."

"But I might get into Berkeley, and a lot of my friends are planning on going there—"

"How many times do I have to tell you you're better than your friends," he said, sneering at the last word.

"That's not true," she said defensively.

"Hal, I thought I lost you." Barbara's mother walked in then, unannounced, still riding on the energy she generated from juggling her busy real estate business with household duties. "There are some bills I want to discuss with you." She looked at Barbara, gave her an absentminded hello, and walked out of the room.

Mr. Vreeland patted Barbara's shoulder before walking out of the room, too.

There was a time, Barbara thought, when she could have gone to her mother for some sympathy about her father's strictness, but during the past few years they hadn't gotten along well with each other at all. Sara Vreeland had been "liberated," as she liked to put it, when Barbara was about ten, and since then, she had single-mindedly pursued her dream of owning her own real estate company. She was totally in agreement with her husband's continual pushing of Barbara to excel at school. But she took things one step further and also discouraged her daughter from taking an interest in boys.

"They'll be plenty of time for them later," she always told Barbara. "I don't want you walking around like a lovesick puppy while you've got your studies to attend to." Barbara had always shrugged off remarks like that, but now she knew—and hoped—that she would get a chance to prove that it was possible to be "lovesick" and not flunk out of school.

After her father left the room, she closed the door and turned the radio back on—quietly this time so it couldn't be heard outside of the room. She listened for a while as Mary Turner interviewed the leader of some new wave band she'd never heard of before. "I bet *your* father let you listen to the radio all the time," she said to the deejay. Taking a look at the physics book, she grimaced and then put it on the edge of her desk. She didn't feel like studying anymore.

Instead, she pulled out the notebook she had buried earlier. There was no way she was going to let her father see what she had been writing in it. Despite her earlier resolve she'd discovered she couldn't get her mind off Michael McNally all evening. It was funny, she thought, thinking of him as a potential boyfriend after so many years of barely tolerating him. Was Kris right about that "layer of contempt" she showed whenever he was around?

All through dinner she had imagined his open, handsome face staring at her from across the dining room table. The expression he wore was the same one she had seen on his face after he had danced with her around the office. Had he, too, she wondered again, felt something special when he held her in his arms?

When she came back up to her room, Barbara did something she had never imagined she would do. She wrote his name all over her notebook, just like Kris did with a boy she had decided she wanted. Then she did something else she had never done before—on a piece of notebook paper, she wrote her name, a plus sign, then Michael's name. Then she wrote "Barbara Vreeland McNally." Seeing the names together gave her a little shiver. It was as if by writing them down, she was putting in motion a series of events that might turn this little fantasy into something real.

She tried to think of reasons why a relationship with him was impossible. For one thing, she really couldn't imagine someone as good looking as he wanting her. She knew she wasn't the only one who thought Michael's black curly hair, deep blue eyes, and wide smile, complete with dimples, very attractive. He kept his six-foot-tall body in shape by playing on the soccer team. He didn't have big muscles, but she thought guys with big muscles were gross anyway.

Michael's sweet face was coupled with a friendly, outgoing personality—with everyone but her, it seemed. He was always talking to someone, she realized, whether at the *Call* or in her economics class, the only one they shared this year. But he hardly ever had a nice word to say to her. Barbara traced it all the way back to kindergarten when she gave him bruised shins in a fight over who was going to use the wooden building blocks. In everything since, from their first grade battle over gold stars to their science project to their work on the *Call*, they seemed to be at cross-purposes, each trying to show the other who was best.

Still, Barbara couldn't help but feel that something had happened between them at the *Call* today, and that as far as she was concerned, nothing would ever be the same between them again. This time reason had nothing at all to do with her feelings.

Before she got ready for bed, she stood by the full-length mirror on the back of her door, inspecting herself. She concluded she had nothing to be ashamed of—she wasn't a knockout, but she had good features. True, she was a little heavier in the thighs than she'd like, but some exercising could take care of that. Everything else about her was well proportioned. Her face was pretty in a quiet way. She liked to think her eyes were her best feature. Wide and deep brown, she liked to think they radiated a kind of mystery. All in all, she wasn't too bad, she thought.

She got ready for bed, then turned down the covers and crawled into bed. Yes, she concluded before drifting off to sleep, she would like to know Michael in a different way. But how she was going to do it, she didn't know.

Chapter 4

The Clear Lake High music room, home base for the hundred-piece marching band and the school orchestra, was located in a separate wing on the east side of the school. Two days later Barbara stood pacing near the door of this room waiting for Kris to join her inside for the senior prom committee meeting.

Barbara was a little nervous. Most of the time she got along with different groups, but when she had to face something like this for the first time, she always felt scared. The committee, dominated by P.K. and jock types, could be kind of intimidating. But, she reasoned, they were the same kids she saw in classes everyday; once the meeting got started, she would calm down and lose her feeling of nervousness.

Finally Kris rounded the corner, red faced from having run down the long green cinderblock corridor.

"Where've you been? You look awful."

"Gee, thanks," Kris said. "Mrs. Kelly kept me after class to go over my history essay. And, as you know, that class is all the way over on the other side of the building, so I had to run all the way over to get here in time. And that's the thanks I get?"

"Sorry," Barbara said. "Look, we've got a few minutes. Let's get you into the bathroom."

Kris bent over the mirror in the girls' room down the hall, repairing her makeup while Barbara watched.

"Boy, it's a good thing Rob won't be at this meeting. He'd die if he saw me like this."

"If he likes you what difference does it make?"

"Barbara," Kris said exasperatedly, brushing on pink eye shadow, "we're just at the getting-to-know-you stage. I'm not ready for him to see me *au naturel.*"

"But it's okay if he's a wreck, right?"

"What can I tell you—life's unfair."

"I wouldn't worry if I were you," Barbara said, straightening out her hair with her fingers. "You look better already."

Kris smiled. "Good. Ready to enter the lion's den?"

"Do you really think they'll be tough? I'm nervous enough as it is."

"Relax. I'm here to give you moral support."

Barbara didn't feel any more relaxed as she poked her head into the music room. Already there were close to thirty seniors inside, and the first ones she spotted were a couple of guys from the wrestling team who'd been cool to her since the hassle over their missing article. Barbara said hello as she went to find a seat, but they ignored her.

Standing next to the teacher's desk was Joanne La Flore, head of the prom committee. Although she was overweight, she had been voted best-dressed senior girl. If she lost those pounds, Barbara thought, she might have been voted best looking as well. She had beautiful blond hair, and her cobalt blue eyes were dazzling. Joanne took her best-dressed title seriously, Barbara thought. Today she was wearing a purple sweater over winter-white pants, and she had on a pair of purple suede boots.

Barbara couldn't help but feel drab compared to Joanne, even though there was nothing wrong with the way she looked in her light green boat-neck shirt and tan jeans.

"Sometimes I feel sorry for Joanne. People mostly notice what she's wearing—and not what she's like," Barbara said.

"C'mon, Barbara. Brian Adams sees a lot in her—or maybe he just sees her a lot." Kris groaned at her own joke.

"Did I hear my name?"

Barbara and Kris turned around slowly and looked into the smiling face of Brian Adams, the tall blond boy who had led Clear Lake's football team to the regional finals this past season. "Hi, there," Barbara said, a red blush rising to her cheeks. "We were just talking about how long you and Joanne have been together."

"Yeah, she's some girl, isn't she?" he said, taking the seat behind them. He whistled admiringly while the girls sighed in relief.

Joanne, who had been busily talking to Denise Morrison, one of her Sigma Epsilon Chi sisters, looked up. She smiled at Brian and waved, but her hand stopped in midair as she made eye contact with Barbara. The smile faded a little, and Joanne quickly turned around and whispered something into Denise's ear.

She's talking about me, Barbara thought with a trace of satisfaction. She was now glad she had come to the meeting. If nothing else she'd at least add another viewpoint to the prom committee proceedings. Looking around now, she noticed that the room was packed with P.K. types. She thought they sometimes acted as if they actually owned the school. Over the years they had managed to take control of social activities like the prom—at first because no one else wanted to, now because they had intimidated everyone else into believing they were the only ones qualified. Barbara, of course, felt they were wrong.

But not every P.K. girl was so conceited. Angela and Amy, identical twins who were old friends of Barbara's, sat down next to her. They chatted briefly, and both were surprised and pleased that someone outside of the usual group had decided to join the committee.

Suddenly a commotion broke out in the back of the room.

"Lisa!" Joanne and Denise squealed in unison, running toward the door.

A small crowd was beginning to gather around the tall, blond cheerleader in the red satin Sigma jacket. Beaming, Lisa proudly displayed the small but perfectly shaped diamond on the third finger of her left hand.

"Lisa, it's beautiful," Joanne gushed.

"Isn't it? Scott picked it out. I love it," she responded giddily.

"What a surprise!" Denise said. "When did he propose?"

"New Year's Eve, but we wanted to keep it a secret until we got the ring," Lisa bubbled. "Not telling anyone was the hardest thing I've ever had to do."

"When are you getting married?" Amy asked excitedly.

"Sometime this summer. Scott feels it's best we both graduate first."

"Oh, brother," Barbara whispered to Kris. They remained in their seats, watching the activity around Lisa. "Are they really going through with it?"

"What's the matter?" Kris asked, waving her congratulations to Lisa, who was making her way to a chair near the kettle drums in the back. "Isn't it romantic?"

"I guess so," Barbara said, smiling in Lisa's direction. "But do they have any idea what they're getting into? The responsibilities, the bills. There's a good chance they'll be divorced within a year."

"Spoilsport," Kris said.

"You mean you don't see anything wrong with a couple of seventeen-year-olds getting married?"

"They'll be eighteen by summer," Kris corrected. "Anyway, they're in love."

"You're hopeless," Barbara said.

Joanne had walked to the front of the room and was now focusing her attention on the other newcomer to the meeting.

"Why, Barbara Vreeland," she said with false sweetness. "What brings you here? Covering the meeting for the *Call*?"

"No," Barbara said, looking directly into Joanne's eyes. "I'm here to participate."

Joanne looked skeptical. "Oh, really?"

"Why not? I though this committee was open to all seniors."

"It is," Joanne admitted. "I just didn't think *you* would be interested."

"Well, I am," Barbara said flatly.

"Then be our guest," Joanne answered, giving Barbara a smile that was a little too sweet.

Then she turned away from Barbara. "Hey, gang, let's get this meeting rolling," she said. "We've got lots of things to cover."

For the next five minutes the room continued to buzz, however, as arriving latecomers swarmed over Lisa and admired her new ring.

Barbara and Kris watched with undisguised amusement as Joanne tried to call the meeting to order. Her gentle persuasion was having no effect.

"Quiet!" Everyone in the room looked up to see Barbara standing near her seat. She had finally grown a little too impatient waiting and felt she had to do something. Her eyes met Joanne's for a moment, and Barbara couldn't miss the glare of contempt in them. It didn't help matters any that her unexpected cry *did* quiet down the room. She smiled innocently and sat down while Joanne continued on with the meeting.

If Barbara had turned her head a little more to the left, she would have seen Michael sitting there, a proud smile on his face.

The next morning Barbara was awakened by the shrill ring of her telephone. Groggily she rolled over to focus on the alarm clock she kept on her night table. Seven-fifteen. Who in their right mind would call in the middle of the night? she wondered. It was a standing rule among her friends that Saturday was her day to sleep in. Must be a wrong number, she thought, turning back onto her stomach.

But the persistent rings wouldn't stop. Barbara turned over again and decided the best thing to do would be to put the phone out of its misery.

"I'm not here!" she mumbled into the receiver. She was about to put the phone back in its cradle when she heard, "Don't hang up. I've got to talk to you!"

"Kris, is that you?" she asked, moving the phone closer to her ear.

"Don't kill me," Kris said. "I know I'm taking a chance, but I've got to talk to you."

"What's wrong?" she asked, gradually coming to life. She thought she could hear Kris crying on the other end.

"Barbara, it was awful," Kris got out before being overcome by a new wave of tears.

"What happened?" Then, remembering, she said, "Your date with Rob, right? Come over to the window."

Following an age-old practice, Barbara put down the phone and got out of bed. Pulling down her nightshirt, she grabbed the phone again and made her way to the window. Looking out she could see Kris standing by the window in her room.

"What went wrong?" Barbara asked. Moving her doll out of the way, she sat down on the window seat.

Kris sighed. "I'm better now." Barbara could see her putting down a tissue. "It was a disaster from moment one. That guy was an animal."

"Oh, boy."

"He made it very clear from the time I got in his car that if I didn't put out for him he wasn't interested."

"But you hardly even know him."

"I know. I thought he was only kidding. But he took me to the drive-in, and it wasn't because of the movie. I thought I could talk him out of it, but it was useless."

"What did you do?"

"What else could I do. I—"

"Kris, you didn't!"

Kris looked at Barbara indignantly. "Of course I didn't! I made a scene and demanded he take me home. I cried for hours when I got back."

"Poor Kris, I'm sorry," Barbara said, looking up. She tried to imagine what her friend had gone through, wondering what she would have done if she had been in her place. "You did the right thing, though."

"I deserved what I got," Kris said glumly.

"Don't think that!" Barbara shouted into the phone. "You didn't do anything wrong, he did."

"No, I mean I built Rob into something he wasn't. I should know better than to go rushing into things."

"Don't be so hard on yourself."

"You know what really gets to me," she said, her tears now gone. "I already had him picked out as prime prom material. Now what will I do?"

Barbara couldn't get over the way Kris always managed to change gears so easily. "But

41

it's only January, and the prom's not till the end of May!"

"It's never too early to make plans," Kris said. "The good ones go so fast."

"I'm not even thinking of anyone yet. I really must be out of it."

"There's always Michael. . . ."

Barbara could see the impish grin on Kris's face and was ready to strangle her. "You got me up in the middle of the night to tell me that?"

"He seemed pretty glad to see you at the meeting yesterday. I saw the way he looked at you."

"Since when does that mean anything?"

"And remember the way he put down Jo-anne when she tried to keep you from speaking? She looked like she was about to kill him afterward."

"She deserved it."

"But did you see the look he gave you after the vote? Something's there, Barbara, I tell you."

"In case you hadn't noticed, he was also giving Marcy Mitchell a lot of looks. They left the meeting together."

"Oh, they're just friends."

"How do you know?"

"She's too much of a fuzzbrain to last long with him."

"I'll tell him the next time I see him. Anyway, none of it matters," she lied. "It's possible I'll decide not to go to the prom at all."

"And I'll join a convent. Oh, come on. You joined the prom committee, and now you're not even planning to go?"

"One thing doesn't have anything to do with the other. You know why I joined."

"And you got what you wanted. The prom's in the gym now. You can quit now if you want to."

"Not so fast. There's still plenty of work to be done."

"Like working on the decorating committee with Michael?"

"He had nothing to do with it."

"Liar," Kris said.

"Really, he didn't. I didn't even know he was the head of the decorating committee till later. I just thought it would be fun to work on the decorations."

"And he had nothing to do with it? Not one little thing?"

"Okay, I was glad to find out he was on the committee," Barbara admitted. "Just a little."

"I thought so," Kris said, smiling. "It's nice to know you have feelings like the rest of the human race."

"Like the rest of the human race, I need my sleep. If you don't mind, I'll see you later."

Barbara put down the phone after saying goodbye and crawled back into the warm security of her bed. She had finally admitted she was interested in Michael but hadn't dared to tell

Kris that the interest was more like a full-blown crush. She knew Kris would blow it way out of proportion and make her very embarrassed. She would keep it to herself for the time being—until she figured out a way to let Michael know how she felt. If she could.

Chapter 5

The following Monday morning, the third period senior class taught by Mr. Matthew Rozzo was waiting anxiously for the arrival of the young economics teacher. All the girls cast thinly disguised glances at the boys, all of whom were sizing up the girls, trying to determine who would be their partner for the next phase of this class.

"Who do you think you're going to get?" Kris asked Barbara.

"I don't know, I haven't given it much thought," she answered, trying to sound aloof.

"Barbara Vreeland," she scolded, "for the next four months you're going to have to pretend you're married to a guy, and you haven't even wondered who it'll be?"

Barbara blushed. She was expecting Kris to say something about Michael, who sat two seats to the back and to the right of her. Of course she had been wondering if she'd be paired with him, but she had concluded there was no way that would happen. Mr. Rozzo had had them fill out questionnaires designed to match up people with common interests, so there was no way she'd get him. "Okay, big mouth, who's your dream man?"

"Mr. Rozzo. He's so gorgeous," Kris said, teasing. Then, looking around the room, she added, "I'd settle for either Mitch, Ron, or Mark."

"I see your broken heart is mended."

"Rob?" Kris asked. "That was ages ago."

Five minutes after the bell rang, Mr. Rozzo entered the room. He had engineered his tardiness on purpose, knowing how much his students were looking forward to this project. He liked to keep them on edge.

The slight, dark-haired teacher was carrying a small leather case in his right hand. With deliberate slowness he raised the case onto his desk and opened it. Inside was a shiny brass bugle, borrowed from the music room for the occasion. Raising it to his lips, Mr. Rozzo tooted out an offkey though effective fanfare while the class stared at him dumbfounded.

"Attention! Attention!" he said, putting down the instrument. "The moment you've all been waiting for is here. Today you will begin the most important project of your high school careers. Get ready, though, 'cause *it could change your life*." He put such a stress on those last five words that some of the students started to laugh nervously.

Barbara shifted in her seat and smiled anxiously at Kris, who did the same. Through the corner of her eye she could also see Joanne, who seemed to be looking in Barbara's direction. Barbara turned to her, smiled, and then turned her head back to the teacher.

"Now, people," Mr. Rozzo continued, using his favorite expression, "you are about to begin a project that will teach you how to handle your lives out there." He pointed to the window. "I've spent the first part of this year telling you everything I know about our economy and how it works. Now I'm going to give you a chance to put all that knowledge to practical use." Turning around to the blackboard, he picked up a piece of chalk and in big block letters wrote: LIFE MANAGEMENT.

Turning around, Mr. Rozzo continued. "Some of you people may be asking yourself: what is life management? What is this crazy guy trying to poison my mind with now? Those of you who know people who were in my class last year or the year before already know the answer. Those of you who have been paying attention in class up to now also know the answer. But for the benefit of those friendless few who have been sleeping through the first half of the school year, I will explain it once again.

"Our educational system was set up to teach you people how to function in the world. It is a task at which it has failed miserably. This modest little exercise," he said, clasping his hands, "is my humble attempt to correct this

47

shortcoming. By the time this project is completed, everyone of you will understand how to run a household, how to keep a budget, how to manage your money, and how to plan your life. In the process I hope you will also learn the fine art of how to get along with others. As you all know I'm having all of you conduct this project with a partner in a 'simulated marriage'—to use the textbook expression."

Everyone looked expectantly around the room again. As Mr. Rozzo went on to explain, every couple would act out four months of a real-life married situation. They would pretend to have jobs and pretend to live on the actual incomes they could expect to have from those jobs. To make it more interesting, each couple would start out with a baby, as well. Once every two weeks they would pick out a "chance" card, which would introduce some unexpected variable into the budget, such as illness, unemployment, change of job, or some other added expense. The object was to see if they could could run their household successfully without going bankrupt.

"Through a lucky coincidence, we have an equal number of males and females in this class. As you know, the questionnaires I had you fill out last week were run through the school computer, so if anyone is unhappy with whom they get, blame the computer not me. I've retired from the matchmaking business. Please be quiet as I read off the list of newlyweds."

When the economics teacher had begun the course two years before, he thought he knew his students well enough to try to pair them up himself, but that strategy hadn't worked well. The next year he had used computer matchups and was more successful.

As Mr. Rozzo went down the list, Barbara mentally crossed off the boys she was sure not to get. Definitely not jock types like John Rush or Mitch Tuckleman from the football team. Or Scott Mecham from the basketball team, whom Mr. Rozzo had already teamed up, naturally enough, with his fiancée Lisa Gardella. Barbara was just about to cross off Mark Sears, a blond-haired swimmer, when she heard his name called off with Kris's. From the smile on her friend's face, Barbara knew she was pleased with the selection. In fact, Barbara was so busy trying to eliminate names for herself that she almost missed hearing Mr. Rozzo call out, ". . . Barbara Vreeland and Michael McNally."

He's got to be kidding, she thought. Or maybe the computer malfunctioned. How could she have ended up with him? Slowly she turned her head toward Michael's back-row seat. He winked slyly at her and gave his best smile.

After Mr. Rozzo finished the roll call, he said, "I hope everyone is pleased. You have five minutes to get to know one another before it's time for your marriage ceremonies."

For the next few minutes there was great commotion in Room 106 at Clear Lake High as everyone sought out their new "spouses." As soon as Mr. Rozzo finished speaking, Kris went right over to Mark before Barbara even had a chance to say congratulations. Barbara, meanwhile, stood by her seat waiting for Michael to come to her, while Michael stood by his seat waiting for her to come to him. Eventually Michael relented and walked to her side.

Taking her hand in his, he said, "Hey, cheer up. Today's your wedding day."

Barbara smiled, trying to hide her shock. "I'm honored." She meant it seriously, but somehow it came out sounding a little sarcastic.

"You could have gotten stuck with Benji," he whispered, pointing.

They both glanced at the pimply faced bespeckled boy who was standing awkwardly next to a very upset Joanne. "You're cruel," she said to Michael. "But *you* could have gotten Joanne." She'd have given anything to have been able to read Joanne's mind at that point. They were even more unlikely a matchup than she and Michael were.

"So you're not disappointed?" he asked.

"It should be interesting," she said noncommittally.

"I guess we must have more in common than we thought. We'll have to compare notes later."

"You're not disappointed, are you?" she asked tentatively.

"With my old lab partner, Felix? Heck no.

50

We're going to have the best marriage of anyone in the class, right?"

"Right," she said hopefully.

"Okay, people," Mr. Rozzo called. "Will you all stand next to your partners?" As everyone got in place, he tapped out the first four notes to "Here Comes The Bride." Putting the bugle down he continued. "I want to begin by asking all of you to please apologize to your parents for not having invited them. Maybe next time. Now will the boys please place the girls' hands in theirs?

"We are all gathered here to learn about life, to join together in unofficial matrimony. Do you all promise to work with your partner, to co-operate, to share, to communicate, to help each other for the next four months?"

"I do," the class said in unison.

"Then I now pronounce you—economically speaking—husbands and wives. You may all shake hands. No kissing in class is allowed."

This time Barbara's clasp was strong and secure. Michael smiled and then whispered to her, "Let's meet after school to talk about this."

Barbara was just about to tell him no, that she had to get home and study, but then thought better of it. "Okay," she answered brightly.

"People, listen," Mr. Rozzo called out. "Back to your seats. I'm going to hand out the ground rules for this project plus budget forms. Your assignment by Friday is to work out your professions, your salaries, and a basic budget. Good luck and much happiness in your new wedded lives."

Barbara looked back again at Michael and thought, maybe one of my dreams might come true. But it was much too early to tell.

Chapter 6

That afternoon Barbara and Michael were sitting in a booth at Emilio's, a local pizza parlor, about to begin their first day of "married" life.

Barbara had never been in Emilio's with a boy, although when she was younger she and Kris had come there every couple of weeks for a pizza dinner with their parents. During the after-school hours, the place was jammed with kids from Clear Lake. Barbara and Michael were lucky to get a booth without waiting.

"Boy, am I hungry," Michael said. "What do you want?"

"A slice and a diet cola," Barbara replied.

"Dieting, are we?"

"A girl is never too young to watch her waistline," she said, in her best imitation of Joanne.

"The editor has a sense of humor after all," he said, surprised, as he rose from the imitation red leather booth.

As she waited for Michael to return with

their food, Barbara glanced around the place. It had changed a lot since she had last been there. The counter near the front had been a recent addition, built solely to serve the after-school crowd. It seemed to Barbara that just about every other boy standing by the counter was wearing a jacket emblazoned with either a Howlers or Ravens insignia. They were the two Clear Lake boys' clubs. Although lots of other kids came to Emilio's, it was a favorite hangout for these groups, and Michael was a Raven. If Michael hadn't been with her, she really would have felt out of place.

Michael, standing at the counter, ordered the food and then looked back at her and smiled. He really is handsome, she thought, admiring his thin, taut body and the way his jeans and rugby shirt seemed to fit him as though they were made especially for him. But it was his smile that really captivated her, a smile that promised so much happiness. Barbara thanked the computer for putting them together. If Kris was right about Michael, that he liked her, everything would be perfect.

Her thoughts were broken by the sounds of food being set on the table.

"I hope you like pepperoni. I thought you might like some on your slice," Michael said. "And anyway, you don't look like some would ruin your diet."

"Pepperoni's fine," she said. "I'll just go light on dinner tonight." It wasn't so much that Barbara dieted, it was that she wasn't used to snacking like this after school. She didn't want to tell that to Michael, however, figuring he'd think she was strange.

"I was just thinking," he said. "I've known you since I was five, and I realize I don't know all that much about you—outside of school stuff, that is."

"I think by the time this project is done you may know more about me than you want to know," she said, biting into the hot pizza. A little glob of cheese slid off the slice and onto her chin. Self-consciously she wiped it off with a napkin.

"I see you're a sloppy eater. It doesn't fit the image."

"What image?"

Michael tore a bite off his slice, wiping off the excess sauce around his lips with his tongue. "Oh, you know, on top of the situation most of the time."

Barbara listened curiously. "There's a lot more to me than that. It's just very hard to be Miss Super Laid Back when I've got so much on my mind."

"Like what?" Michael asked.

Barbara told him about the pressures her father and mother put on her to get good grades and get into a good school. "My father says all this work will build up my character," she concluded. "But what good is character if you can't have any fun?"

Michael had listened to her story with concern. He admired how she was able to handle it all. "Maybe we'll have some fun working on this project, Mrs. McNally." He winked playfully.

"I still can't believe the computer matched us together, Mr. Vreeland," she said pointedly.

"I've been thinking. . . . It's not so strange. We both work on the paper, right?"

Barbara nodded.

"And we're both on the prom committee," he said, counting off on his fingers. "And we both like pizza and the color blue." He pointed to their matching tops. "See, we have a lot in common."

"If that's so true," Barbara wondered, "how come it's always been easier for us to fight than to talk to each other?"

"Maybe because we're both stubborn and used to getting our own way. That's another thing we have in common. But we'll show 'em this time, right?" He raised his soda can. "A toast. To the best partnership in the whole class."

Barbara hit her plastic cup against his can. "Shall we get started then?"

"Anything you say."

"The first thing we have to decide on is our jobs. What do you want to be when you grow up?" she asked.

"A plumbing supplies salesman," he answered.

Barbara almost choked on her soda. "You're

kidding!" But she quickly stifled her laughter when she saw that Michael was serious.

"Really. My dad owns a plumbing supply business, which I'm going to take over someday. I know it sounds funny, but it happens to be one of the largest in the valley."

"I'm impressed."

"And what are your plans?" he asked seriously.

"I'm hoping to get into Berkeley or Stanford—that's where my dad wants me to go—and major in journalism. I'm going to be a reporter."

"On TV?"

"Maybe. Though my dad would like me to follow in his footsteps."

"But what would *you* like?"

"I'm not sure. I'm leaning toward newspaper work now, but I'm going to learn more about TV news in college. I figure at this point I'm ahead of the game just knowing what I want to do with my life. Most everybody I know hasn't the faintest idea."

"I know." Michael pulled a pencil out of his jacket and rapped it on the table in mock imitation of a teletype machine. "And now for the top story of the day," he said in the low tones of a radio announcer. "We have just learned that Barbara Vreeland, ace L.A. reporter, has been awarded the Pulitzer Prize for the best news story of the year."

In spite of herself, Barbara blushed. "You're crazy, Michael."

"No, just having fun." He put the pencil away, then took her hand in his. "I figure if I'm going to be married to a reporter, she's just got to be the best there is. Know what I mean?"

"I'm surprised you're not considering journalism yourself. You're really good," she noted.

"You really think so?" he asked, taking his hand away from hers to pick up his soda can.

"You sound surprised."

"I am. I thought you didn't like my stuff."

"Well I do—even if I never said so before."

"Thank you."

"You're welcome. So have you decided on a college yet?"

"I'd be just as happy to go to Cal State and work with my dad part time, but my parents are pushing me into going to Berkeley. I haven't decided yet."

"Berkeley may not be such a bad idea." For an instant she had a vision of them both walking hand in hand on the beautiful campus.

"That's what they keep telling me. But there's no surfing up there." He laughed.

"I think we'd better get back to the project," she said.

Barbara was sure that the feelings coming over her now were the result of Michael's closeness and it scared her more than she wanted to admit. It was much easier—and safer for now—to stick to school matters.

"The way I see it," he said, "all we have to do

is find out the typical first-year salaries for our jobs. Sounds easy enough."

"Sure, you ask your dad, and I'll ask mine. But we have to go apartment hunting, too."

"Huh-uh." He shook his head.

"And why not?"

"Apartments are too confining. I've always wanted a beach house."

"I imagine they're pretty expensive," she noted.

"So what? This is a pretend marriage, so let's have a pretend beach house."

"You're forgetting we have to pretend to be able to afford it on the basis of the real going rates."

"We've got two salaries, right?" he countered.

"I don't know about the plumbing business, but I'm pretty sure the big money in journalism doesn't come till you're in it for a while. Don't expect a fat paycheck from my end."

"I'd like to check into it anyway."

"Fine with me. Just remember, we've got a baby," she added. "They cost money, too."

Michael knitted his brow. "How are you going to work if you've got to take care of a kid?"

"We'll take care of the kid together," she stressed. "We'll have to add the cost of a baby-sitter to our budget." She got out her notebook and began to jot down some notes.

Michael sighed. "Being an adult is a little more complicated than I thought."

"That's why Mr. Rozzo's having us do this. You know, a heavy dose of reality."

"I would like to stay a teenager a little while longer if you don't mind," he said, taking another sip of soda. "Scott and Lisa have got to be nuts to want to tie themselves down like this."

"Not into making commitments, huh?"

"Not now. I suppose I might get married someday, but I want to live a little first."

"I know what you mean."

Michael nodded. "Little Miss Independence."

Barbara was disturbed by the tone of his voice. "Is there anything wrong with that?"

"Don't get me wrong," he said quickly. "I think it's great for a girl to be independent. That's a lot more appealing than a girl who clings."

Barbara was encouraged by Michael's remarks. In his own way he was saying he liked her!

After a brief silence, Michael shifted in his seat and said, "I think it's great that you're working on the decorating committee."

"Sounds like fun."

"If it's anything like the junior prom one, it will be. But are you sure your father will let you do it?"

"He doesn't seem to mind anything if it's school related. But I could get grounded for a while if I get anything lower than a B-plus on my report card."

"It must be tough having a dad that strict."

"My mom's not much better," she complained. "Sometimes I wish I had a brother or sister so I'd have someone to share the load with."

"I don't know." Michael shook his head. "My little brother can be a real pain sometimes."

They went on like that for the next few minutes, chatting aimlessly about their families. Barbara hadn't realized that Michael's mother had died when he was little and that the woman she always thought of as his mother was actually his stepmother. It made her realize she had a lot to learn about him.

"Say, Barb, have you made any plans for the prom yet?" he asked suddenly.

Is he going to ask me? she thought in a sudden burst of anticipation. In a flash she pictured herself walking into the gym on Michael's arm. For some reason she saw herself dressed in a pale blue chiffon gown—the kind of dress she had never before dreamed she'd wear.

"Not yet. Why?"

If he heard the anticipation in her voice, he ignored it. "I'm just trying to figure out girls," he said vaguely. "You mind if I ask you something?"

"Depends on what it is."

"You may think it's funny of me to be

61

asking you this, but this is something that I'd like to get a girl's opinion on. Do you think it's important for a guy to ask a girl to the prom months in advance?"

"It's funny you mention that. Kris was just telling me how the race to get dates is on."

"But do you think there's something strange about a guy wanting to wait before committing himself to a girl?"

"Depends on who the girl is and how much he cares about her," she said flatly, realizing that he wasn't going to ask her to the prom.

"I'm getting a lot of pressure from a girl right now. Marcy Mitchell. You know her?"

Barbara's heart froze at the mention of the girl's name. "I've seen her around."

"I've gone out with her a couple of times, and she's kinda got it into her head that we're going together—which we're definitely not. I mean she's okay, but a lot could happen between now and the prom. I'd hate to commit myself so soon."

"So don't ask her."

"If I don't, someone else might grab her, and then I'd be out of luck."

"Why are you telling me this?" she asked, growing increasingly uneasy.

"Because you seem to care. And it's hard to talk about this kind of thing with a guy. Everybody I know would kill to be in my shoes."

"Look, I've got to go," she said suddenly,

hiding behing a false smile. "I'll see you tomorrow."

"Sure thing," he said, not realizing how his words had hurt her.

Quickly Barbara rose from the table and hurried out of the pizza parlor. The tears that she had struggled so hard to hold back while Michael was pouring out his heart to her now began to flow freely as she approached her car and got inside. She fumbled with her keys, trying to find the one for the ignition, finally throwing the bunch down on the passenger's seat in frustration. Putting her head on the steering wheel, she sat and cried, hoping that no one would notice. Independent. That's all he wanted her to be, she thought, hurt and saddened that nothing more was there. She realized she couldn't blame him—he had no idea what was going on inside her. But just being his friend wasn't enough for her anymore. She should have been satisfied with the day's accomplishments—after all, just last week they had been sniping adversaries. But Barbara had created a lovely dream, in which Michael would suddenly discover her and, like some Prince Charming, carry her off.

I'm such a fool, she thought, sobbing. Just when I fall for a guy, he turns out to have a steady girl. Wiping away the tears as she started the car, Barbara felt sad and confused. Was she much better off sticking to her studies and her work on the paper? Was it better to feel "safe"— and lonely? And anyway, how could she stop feeling the ache that Michael's words had caused? And what about the "Prince Charming" dreams? Barbara's tears seemed to blur even her thoughts as she headed home.

Chapter 7

"I want a divorce," Barbara told Mr. Rozzo the next morning before class.

"Barbara, the project just started. You can't be having problems already."

"No," she said. "I just think the computer made a mistake. I'd feel more comfortable if I had someone else to work with." She couldn't tell Mr. Rozzo her real reason for wanting the switch—that now that she knew Michael had another girl, it would be impossible for her to pretend to be married to him.

"Have you discussed this with Michael?" the teacher asked.

"No. Could I have someone else?" she asked again. "Please?"

Mr. Rozzo looked at her critically. "I'm surprised, Barbara. Of all the students in my class, you're the last one I'd ever expect to complain."

"So you'll make the switch?" she asked eagerly.

"Out of the question," Mr. Rozzo said emphatically. "Whatever problems you have with

Michael you're going to have to work out with him. Understand?"

"Yes, Mr. Rozzo," she said dejectedly. She turned and sat down in her seat just as the late bell rang, dropping her books on the top of the desk with a thud.

Fortunately she didn't have to look at Michael while Mr. Rozzo presented his talk about budget planning, explaining the sheets he had handed out the day before. She welcomed the chance to concentrate on her note taking, writing carefully, making her handwriting neat and legible. And when the bell at the end of the period rang, she ran out of the room before Michael had a chance to say a word to her.

But Barbara couldn't avoid Michael completely that day. The first meeting of the senior prom decorating committee was that afternoon in the auditorium. Barbara seriously considered not going, dawdling by her locker after her last class let out. But she told herself she had made the commitment and had to see it through. So slowly she walked over to the auditorium, arriving there just two steps ahead of Michael.

"Hey, Mrs. McNally," he said pleasantly.

She pretended not to hear him, but Michael followed her through the door anyway. "If I didn't know better, I'd swear you were avoiding me," he said to her back.

"I was doing nothing of the kind," she said

flatly. "And my name's not Mrs. McNally. We didn't get marriage certificates yesterday." In a futile effort to outpace him, she walked briskly down to the front row of seats, where the other committee members were sitting.

"Sorry, I forgot you're not into nicknames. Anyway, I'm glad I was wrong. From the way you left Emilio's yesterday, I thought I'd done something to make you mad."

"Why should I be mad at you?" she asked.

"Beats me," he said as he jumped onto the stage. He sat down, straddling his feet over the edge. Counting heads and then looking at his watch he said, "Looks like we're all here. I'm going to turn the meeting over to Joanne, who'll explain what we're all going to do for the next few months. Joanne?"

Joanne took her place at the foot of the stage, standing before the dozen or so seniors on the committee. She talked at length about the prom, excitedly predicting how it was "going to be the best prom in Clear Lake's history," and how everyone on the committee had to pledge to work their hardest to pull it off.

Barbara listened, with a mixture of cynicism and awe, to Joanne's speech. While she found it hard to understand how anyone could get so worked up over a dance, she had to marvel at Joanne's obvious dedication and at the way she managed to excite and inspire everyone in the room—including her, she realized with a start. By the time Joanne had finished, Barbara felt willing to throw herself into any task the committee wanted her to do.

Even as Joanne was speaking, however, Barbara found herself casting furtive glances at Michael. It was going to be very hard to shut off her feelings for him, she realized. Emotions weren't like a water faucet that could be shut off at will. They were more like a stream, continually flowing. The only way to stop a stream's flow, she concluded, was to build a dam. And she would have to build a dam around her own heart, hardening her attitude to Michael. If he stopped acting nice to her, she reasoned, it would be a lot easier to forget she ever felt anything good about him.

After Joanne's remarks, the discussion moved toward ways of bringing the prom theme, Love Blossoms Eternally, to life. Everyone liked Joanne's idea of turning the gym into a beach-side lovers' retreat filled with flower blossoms. "And we could get real flowers—maybe even a few palm trees, too—to add to the effect."

"And we could get flowers for all the tables," Lisa added excitedly.

"And maybe leis for all the girls to wear," suggested Kevin Nowak.

"It sounds so romantic," Lisa said.

"Don't fresh flowers cost a lot of money?" Barbara wondered aloud.

Joanne scowled at her. "That's why we have

a fund-raising committee," she snapped back.

"Now wait," Michael stepped in. "Barbara does raise a good point. Sure, we'll raise the money for the decorations, but we want to make sure we get our money's worth. I think we should have someone investigate."

"Not a bad idea," Kevin said. A few of the others voiced their agreement.

"Good. Since Barbara has shown an interest in this matter, I suggest we let her do it. Any objections?"

There were none.

"Okay with you, Barbara?"

"Sure," she answered flatly, remembering her pledge. But she wondered when she would have the time.

"Good. Anybody else have some decorating suggestions?" he asked the group.

The discussion rambled on for another half hour. Kevin Nowak, one of the senior class's best artists, talked about ways he could dress up the gym. He also offered the idea of constructing two gold-painted papier-mâché Cupids to hover over the scoreboard. Lisa thought the idea was inventive and romantic, though others in the room felt the touch might be too much. Barbara sat silent, not wanting to be accused of standing in the way of romance. In the end, Michael decided to put the suggestion to a vote. The Cupids won.

He adjourned the meeting right after that,

adding, almost as an afterthought, "And, Barbara, you'll have that information about the flowers for us next week?"

She was stunned. With the next issue of the *Call* to be planned and a history report to write, she wasn't sure she could have the information that soon. As the others left the room, she decided to wait and tell Michael when they were alone.

"Now what was the idea of giving me all that work?" she asked him angrily.

"Calm down. What's the problem?"

His casual attitude only fueled her anger. "Calm down! Like I have nothing better to do that spend hours on the phone calling every florist in L.A. County! What do you think I am, a computer?"

Michael rested one elbow on his books. He was surprised to see Barbara so worked up. "I thought you wanted to work on the committee."

"I do. But why am I the one who has to do all the work? You didn't load anyone else with this kind of job."

"You're not like everyone else," he said sincerely.

She blurted out, "I know, you're just getting back at me for complaining to Mr. Rozzo this morning."

Michael's expression was puzzled. "What are you talking about?"

Barbara sucked in her breath, instantly regretting her words. "Oh, nothing," she answered vaguely.

But now his curiosity was piqued. "What did you complain to Mr. Rozzo about?"

"I told you it was nothing. Let's forget it, huh?" She didn't dare tell him what she had done this morning. She would really feel like a fool.

"You're not getting out of this so easily, Barbara," he said, his patience wearing thin. "Why did you complain to Mr. Rozzo about me?"

"It wasn't you," she said hastily. "It was me. I—I told him I had some problems adjusting to the idea of the life management project. It had nothing to do with you."

"I see," he said, unconvinced. "You're playing another one of your power trips, aren't you?"

"Don't be ridiculous. Let's forget it, okay?"

"Not so fast," he said. "I have a feeling you're upset because I'm ordering you around for a change."

"That's silly."

"Is it? It occurs to me, sitting here now, that for the first time in a long time, I'm in a position to give you orders. And you can't take it." He shook his head in amazement.

"You'll have those numbers at next week's meeting, Michael McNally!" she said before storming out of the room. In a way, though, she was just as glad he thought she was on a power trip. It was far more bearable to her at this point than having to admit her true feelings to him.

Chapter 8

"A Porsche is out of the question!" Barbara said firmly.

"But I want it," Michael said.

"It doesn't fit in the budget."

"I'll make it fit," he insisted.

The newlyweds were sitting in Mr. Rozzo's class two weeks later, trying to work out the latest problem in the life management project. They had just picked their first "chance" card, which read: *Car breaks down. Engine beyond repair. New car needed.* They had until the end of the period to decide on a course of action.

"We can't afford a car that expensive," Barbara repeated, trying to keep her voice calm. She was determined to be all business with Michael, but as far as she was concerned, he was not cooperating at all. He seemed to her to be interested in spending their money as soon as it came in, instead of embarking on the prudent savings plan she had devised. She thumbed through the pages on her desk and pulled out a long list of numbers, hoping she could get Michael to see the picture at last.

Michael was not easily convinced. There was a time, he thought, when he would have been very willing to compromise with her, but it had become increasingly obvious to him that Barbara was only interested in making things difficult for him. It was especially confusing to him, given the ease with which they had seemed to get along that day in Emilio's. But there was a part of him that could be just as stubborn as she, which was why he was being so insistent. Scanning the figures she presented him, he scowled, "So we'll change the budget, that's all."

"We can't," Barbara cried. "We both know how much we're earning. There's no way we'd be able to make payments on a car that expensive."

"What's the big deal?" Michael persisted. "Let's just say my dad gave us the money for the car."

"Just like he gave us the money for the beach house?" she snapped.

That "house" had led to their first disagreement as "husband and wife." Michael had wanted to spend the bulk of their paycheck to cover the rent on that house, while Barbara countered that it would leave practically nothing to pay for food or anything else.

"So I was wrong about that," he admitted. "I

forgot we needed money for Michael, Jr., too."

"How many times do I have to tell you—we have a girl not a boy." The question of their baby's sex had led to their second disagreement. The subject had come up right after Michael had thrust that work on her at the prom committee meeting, and she hadn't been in any mood to capitulate to his desires.

"It's a boy," Michael insisted. "Mr. Rozzo said we could have any kind of baby we wanted, and I want a boy."

"And I want a girl," she said firmly.

"Boy," Michael slammed his fist on the desk.

"Okay, we'll have it your way," she said, thinking that she could still call it a girl if she wanted.

"Great."

Barbara looked at Michael's grinning face. One part of her was now turned off by Michael's stubbornness and extravagance. But another part of her was still undeniably attracted to the person he was outside of class. She shook her head strongly, the practical side of her winning out for now. "It's not right," she told him. "Mr. Rozzo said we have to make do on our own money, not by handouts from anyone else."

"Taking money from my dad is not a handout," he noted.

"For the purpose of this project it is."

"Why? This is supposed to be a course in

real life, right? Well, in real life my dad would give me the money for the car, so why can't I take it now?"

Barbara conceded that he might have a point, but a principle was a principle, and she wasn't about to give in now. "I still say we can't use it. It's not in the rules."

Michael looked at her strangely. "You really take this seriously."

"Don't you?"

He shrugged.

"But it's important, Michael. How can you not take it seriously?" she asked, genuinely puzzled. "You were so enthusiastic when we first started."

"That was before I realized we had to play by such dumb rules. Besides, why should I worry about the future? I'll graduate from high school, go to college, then go into my father's business. Those are the rules I'm playing my life by."

"Well, some people don't have it that easy."

Barbara looked down at the desk and shuffled some of her papers. The part of her that didn't like Michael was winning out—and for some reason she didn't like that.

Things between Michael and Barbara didn't improve all that much during the next two months. She would sit in class attentively, listening to Mr. Rozzo's lectures about financial planning and the need for partners to be very explicit in letting their desires be known to one another. She'd come out of the class, half wanting to follow that advice and work things out with Michael and half realizing that if she let down her guard, the emotions that she had dammed up inside her would be let loose. She hurt enough without letting Michael see it.

In contrast to her relationship with Michael, was Kris's partnership with Mark. They had worked hard on their project from day one and were getting along very well. They worked out their problems rationally. But instead of making Kris happy, it got her frustrated.

"I can't get him interested in me," she complained to Barbara one day in early April. "I know he likes me, and we have a lot of fun together in class, but he won't ask me out!"

"Maybe he's got a girlfriend."

"No, that's the funny thing about it. Working on this project, we've both talked a lot about ourselves, so I know he's not going out with anybody. But the prom is only six weeks away, and I'm getting worried."

"Maybe you should look for someone else."

Kris shook her head. "Mark's different. He's not someone who's in my life one day, out the next. I've actually gotten to know him, and he's something special."

"Maybe you're coming on too strong and scaring him off."

"You think so?"

"Could be. For what it's worth, from what I

could tell he does seem to like you. Give him a little more time."

"That could be hard."

"Is he worth waiting for?"

Kris blushed. "He sure is. Have you been thinking about who you might go to the prom with?"

"Not really."

"You're not still hung up on Michael, are you?"

"Do I seem hung up on him?"

"No. And it's just as well. I heard he finally broke down and asked Marcy Mitchell to the prom."

"Oh," Barbara said noncommittally, though inside she wanted to kill Kris for being so blasé about Michael. Still she realized Kris wasn't to blame. Over the past weeks all she'd done was complain about Michael, so it was only natural for Kris to think she no longer cared for him. But despite everything that had happened, her feelings for Michael were still very much intact.

Two weeks later, at the end of another one of their futile life management discussions, he calmly told her, "By the way, that article you wanted about this project will be on your desk in the morning."

Chapter 9

It wasn't until after school the next day that Barbara had a chance to read Michael's article. As he had told her, it was lying on her desk, held in place with the little brass typewriter paperweight she had received when she was made editor of the *Call*. She was hesitant to pick it up; she had assigned him the article before the two of them were paired, and now she was worried about what he would reveal about their relationship.

After a while, she closed the door, sat down at her desk, and began to read. The first few paragraphs allayed her fears. Michael had begun the article with a humorous account of that first day, and she found herself laughing at the way he had described Mr. Rozzo and his bugle. Michael had a knack for being able to draw a fast, accurate sketch of people and to depict them with wit and style. Although he deliberately didn't use anyone's real name throughout the article, she knew that no one in the class would mistake who he was writing about. It was obvious that the "lovebirds in paradise" he described "as a textbook case for the rationale for this project," were Lisa and Scott. "In the past few weeks there have been rumblings of trouble in their paradise," he wrote, "as they have been forced to come face to face with some of the painful day-to-day realities of marriage." He went on to describe how "Paula," his pseudonym for Lisa, became incensed when "Paul" took away her department store charge card, especially since he had gone out and bought a new stereo system for his car.

Next to Barbara and Michael, Scott and Lisa had had the most problems of any couple in the class. They both spent their money recklessly, without the benefit of generous fathers or well-paying jobs. The project led to more than one out-of-class fight, as it became clear to them what they faced down the road as young marrieds. Barbara wondered if Lisa would give back the ring.

She returned her attention to Michael's article.

This class has taught Clear Lake seniors much about themselves and has produced a few surprises. One is the couple that could be dubbed "least likely to succeed." Jill, a popular, outgoing self-proclaimed party girl was matched up with Jack, a self-proclaimed computer nut and semirecluse, more at home with a microprocessor than a miss. Who would have thought they would have lasted? Yet Jill told this reporter that she and Jack have learned to accommodate each other's interests on their limited budget and have discovered they share a passion for music and video games. "It helps that Jack is one of the kindest and most thoughtful persons I've ever met," she added. Hmm, could this be the start of a real-life romance for these two?

Barbara read this section with amusement. She doubted that Joanne, alias Jill, would be caught dead in public with Benji, aka Jack. Still, their successful partnership had been the biggest surprise of the class. Barbara suspected it might even have something to do with the subtle change in Joanne's attitude she had noticed lately. Joanne had begun to talk civilly to Barbara about the prom, at last realizing that Barbara's commitment to the decorating committee was sincere. Barbara wouldn't exactly say they were great friends now, but for the first time in her life Joanne seemed to acknowledge that the world wasn't populated only with P.K.'s and jocks.

But if Barbara was pleased with Michael's account so far, her expression darkened as she read on.

But for all the success stories to be found, there are some notable failures as well. One couple in particular has proved to be a big disappointment. This couple consists of Oscar, a friendly, gregarious kind of guy, and Felix, a cold, unfriendly kind of girl. From the onset of the project Felix was determined to show that she was the boss. She insisted on making all the decisions, without considering Oscar's opinions. Protests from Oscar notwithstanding, Felix continued to blithely go her own way. Oscar told this reporter that he feels he could cut class for the rest of the year without it making one bit of difference to the project. Oscar adds he's very disappointed, as he thought that through the project he would come to a better understanding of Felix— and possibly much more. He now sees, however, that Felix is a big letdown.

There was more to the article, but Barbara couldn't finish it. She felt a deep, dull ache in the pit of her stomach. There was no mistaking the last account as anything but a thinly disguised version of her last few months with Michael, and it hurt her to see the results of her behavior spelled out in cold black type. She suspected Michael had deliberately slanted the article to make himself look good—after all he wasn't totally blameless, either—but it didn't make her feel any better to know that he now considered her "cold" and "a big letdown."

But another part of what he said really threw her. That was the part he mentioned about being disappointed and having hoped for something better. Had he been expecting something more out of the "marriage"—just as she had? Had she made a big mistake by making more out of his relationship with Marcy than really existed?

The article preyed on Barbara's mind throughout the rest of the afternoon. As soon as she got home she called Kris and asked her to hurry over at once. She had to get a second opinion.

If she was confused when she handed Michael's article to Kris, she was even more puzzled by the time Kris had finished reading it.

Kris had taken the article and plopped down on Barbara's patchwork quilt. She lay on her stomach facing the foot of the bed, her toes resting on the back of pillows at the top. Barbara sat at her desk chair, trying to interpret Kris's expression as she read. Kris's intermittent giggles only made Barbara more anxious.

"This is great stuff," Kris said when she finished.

"Is that all you have to say?"

"I liked the part about Mark and me. Say, your advice may be working. I think he's close to asking me out."

"That's great, Kris. But what did you think about that Felix and Oscar part?"

Kris turned away, hesitating, choosing her words carefully. "It was kind of cute the way he used those names to describe you two."

"You're evading me."

Kris sat up and swung her legs around so they hung over the foot of the bed. "What can I say, Barb. Michael's very perceptive."

"You think he's right? I thought you were my friend."

"I am. It's just very hard to tell a friend she may have some flaws in her character."

"So you think all I want is to make life miserable for him?"

"Of course not," Kris said. "But Michael thinks so, and there's got to be a good reason why. How far off is this article anyway?"

Barbara looked down at the carpet. "Not very," she admitted. "But he's wrong if he thinks I didn't care about his feelings. The problem is I cared too much."

"And you didn't let him know?"

"I was afraid to."

Barbara had been sitting upright against the wooden slats of her chair, but as Kris went on she felt herself automatically slouch down.

"Just look at yourself," Kris said. "You're so wound up you hardly relax. You know how long I've been trying to get you to be more laid back—less uptight about everything?"

"But what about school—and the paper?"

"C'mon Barb, you don't really believe that."

"How can you say that?"

"Because you spend all your time studying to get the same A's you'd get if you studied half as long. I could understand when you were under all that pressure from your dad to get into Stanford, but you've already been accepted there."

"So?"

"So it's something besides work that's spoiled things with Michael. Are you telling me everything?"

Barbara played with her fingers. "I'll never get him to think of me as a girlfriend—the way he does Marcy."

Kris looked at her in amazement. "You think Michael's got a thing for her?"

"He *is* taking her to the prom."

"Out of desperation, I think. I don't even think they're dating anymore."

"No?" Barbara was truly surprised.

Kris threw her hands up in frustration. "I've said it before, and I'll say it again. For a smart kid you're awfully dumb when it comes to boys."

"I was better off when I wasn't even thinking of him. It made life simpler."

"And not nearly as interesting, right?"

"Sometimes I wish I could be more like Miss Gregg. She's bright and attractive and happy. And she's not preoccupied with men."

"That's right—there's only one."

"What do you mean?"

"Where have you been? The biggest news around school is the rumor that she's going out with Mr. Rozzo."

"You're kidding." Barbara's eyes grew wide.

Kris shook her head. "For a newsperson you can be awfully out of it."

Barbara sat silent. "I guess you're right. But what do I do about Michael?"

"From the article I get the impression I was right about him—you did have something he was interested in. Whether or not you've blown it, I can't say, but for starters you can print this article."

"What will that prove?"

"It's possible it's his way of testing you, to see if you can take criticism as well as you can give it."

"And then what?"

"Isn't there something good you can say about him? If you want him you'd better let him know."

"But what if he doesn't want me?"

"It sounds really scary," Kris said, "but I think you've just got to give it a chance."

"And if I lose?"

"Maybe it's better to try—and lose—than not to try at all." She paused. "But if you don't lose—just think—wow!"

Barbara had to admit that Kris had a point. Already she was feeling hopeful about the situation, and in spite of herself she grinned. After a while she said, "You doing anything tonight?"

"Besides talking to you?"

"I mean for the next few hours. I want to go out and celebrate."

"Celebrate what?" Kris looked at Barbara as if she had just announced she was going to jump off a pier.

"The new me," Barbara announced.

"What?"

"Yeah. I figure there's going to be a new me who's got enough nerve to face Michael. And maybe show him that he was right to expect something from me—but that he was wrong to call me 'a big letdown.'"

"I can't believe it's you who's talking."

"I know. But I do have a lot to celebrate. Remember months back how I said I was going to raise the roof the night I got accepted at Berkeley and my parents agreed I could go? And how I ended up here with Macbeth, my doll, and my homework?"

"Yeah, some party that was."

"Well, the 'new me' thinks I should party and celebrate about Berkeley and—"

"And Michael." Kris laughed.

"And Michael." Barbara smiled.

Chapter 10

There was a note waiting for Barbara in her homeroom the next morning. It was from the principal's office, summoning her for a meeting at ten-thirty. Right before her economics class.

Of all the days to call me, she wailed to herself. Now when would she get a chance to talk to Michael? She had spent every second since she had wakened that morning getting up her courage to tell him how his article had affected her. Now she would have to wait another day.

Shortly before ten-thirty, Barbara walked over to the principal's office, still curious about the meeting. Just before going inside she popped into the bathroom nearby to check her appearance. She was glad that for once, at least, she wasn't wearing jeans. Instead, she had on a mauve skirt and vest and a white, mauve, and gray striped shirt. She had worn it especially to impress Michael.

With her head held straight, Barbara opened the glass door that led to the school office.

"Hi, Mrs. Barclay," she said brightly to the secretary at the front desk. "Mr. Hoffman wants to see me?"

The gray-haired secretary nodded and then buzzed the principal's office. "Barbara Vreeland is here, sir." After a pause she said, "Go ahead. He's waiting for you inside."

Uh-oh I'm late, Barbara thought as she walked down the plush gray pile carpet to Mr. Hoffman's office. But the clock on the wall said ten-thirty, and with that worry out of the way, she opened the wood-paneled door and walked inside.

Mr. Hoffman, a short, balding man in his mid-fifties, stood up when she entered. "Hello, Barbara," he said pleasantly. "I'm sure you remember Mr. Goffit, Mrs. Whaney, and Mr. Hayes?"

Barbara smiled politely at the three members of the school board. She had met them once before, at the one school board meeting she'd attended that year. "Yes, it's nice to see you again," she said.

"We're glad you were able to take time out of class to join us," Mr. Goffit, a portly businessman, said.

Barbara could only stare at him blankly. She still had no idea why they wanted to see her.

"Sit down, Barbara," Mr. Hoffman said,

pointing to a green leather chair next to his desk. "We'll try not to keep this meeting too long. We know you want to get back to class."

"Yes, Mr. Hoffman," she said dutifully.

Picking up some papers from his cluttered desk, the principal continued. "These board members want to talk to you about this." He showed her the editorial on pledging she had written back in December.

"What about it?" she asked.

This time it was Mrs. Whaney's turn to speak. A short, wiry woman in her early forties, she had a nasal, high-pitched voice that Barbara found irritating. "Several members of the board, including all of us here, were quite impressed with this editorial. As a matter of fact, we were surprised that a young girl like yourself would have the integrity to write with such forcefulness and conviction about these—I don't know what else to call them—gangs. Over the past few months we've been very upset about their behavior in our schools. They're nothing but troublemakers and social misfits, and they've become a menace, a threat to the other students."

"But Mrs. Whaney," Barbara protested, "there aren't any gangs in our school. I was simply writing about—"

"Now, now," Mrs. Whaney continued. "I know how it is with teenagers, sticking together against us 'old folks' on the board. You don't have to hide the truth."

"I'm not hiding anything," Barbara said, her voice rising slightly.

"You've shown that you're very concerned about these groups," Mr. Goffit continued. "That's why we've asked you to come."

"All I did was complain about the pledging practices of some of the social clubs—"

"We know. And we agree with you that something has to be done about them," Mr. Goffit said. "Next week we're going to submit a proposal to the full board that would ban these gangs from the campus before this situation really gets out of hand. And we'd like you to testify in our behalf."

"But, Mr. Goffit, these clubs aren't gangs. Mr. Hoffman, you know that," she said pointedly.

Mr. Hoffman sat silently, pretending to look for something in the large stack of papers on the side of his desk.

"Barbara, we know you'll do what's right," Mrs. Whaney insisted, ignoring everything Barbara had said.

"And we've prepared some notes you might want to include in your speech to the board," Mr. Goffit continued. He rose to hand her a manila folder.

Barbara felt three sets of eyes staring at her. She was amazed that anyone on the board could have jumped to such a wild conclusion from her editorial—and even more amazed that they didn't want to listen to her explanations. It was as if they had already made up their minds to take action against the clubs and nothing was going to stop them.

"We'll be looking forward to seeing you at the meeting," Mrs. Whaney said.

"Barbara, you may go back to your class now," Mr. Hoffman said brusquely. "The board members thank you for your attendance."

Seeing she had no choice, Barbara backed out of the room. Now she was faced with something she dreaded. She had never wanted to see the clubs banned from school. True, she wasn't crazy about them, but they were practically an institution, almost as old as the school itself. And none of them could be considered a gang by anyone who'd ever seen them. There was no way she could support the board members on this issue. And they certainly hadn't helped their cause by the way they had talked to her. Barbara felt like going back into Mr. Hoffman's office and telling them off, but she knew that that wouldn't help the situation—not in the mood the board was in.

Feeling very confused and angry, Barbara walked back to her economics class. She had only missed half of it, but she wasn't in the mood now to listen to anything Mr. Rozzo had to say. And even more important, she had lost her nerve about talking to Michael. She stood beside the closed door to Room 106 for a few moments before deciding not to go inside.

I just can't face it—and him—right now, she thought, and turned away. Five minutes later she was in front of the *Call* office. She quickly opened the door and made her way to her desk. Turning around to the side table, she picked up a copy of the December issue and reread her editorial.

> Every fall the halls of Clear Lake High are crawling with strange-looking girls with painted faces and boys made to wear the stupidest clothes. It's called pledging, an age-old tradition carried out by this school's social organizations. Some say it's all good fun, but we at the *Call* believe it is a demeaning activity that disrupts the atmosphere of learning that is supposed to be the hallmark of this campus.

Barbara sat at her desk, thinking about the article. Her call for the elimination of open pledging sounded harsh and petty. The entire editorial seemed overdone—nowhere in the whole piece did she cite one valid reason that supported her conclusion that the pledges interrupted the learning process.

She thought back with irony to that day when Michael had chided her for the editorial. He was right to have called it a childish, silly thing to do. Although she still thought that the clubs made some students feel left out, basically the clubs were just a group of kids who got together to have a good time. She also knew that a lot of them, including Joanne's Sigma

Epsilon Chi, did some volunteer work in the community and at the local hospital—and she herself didn't do that.

She also realized now that a lot of the girls, even Joanne, weren't the total airheads she had thought they were. She had come to grudgingly admire Joanne for the way she was working to put the prom together. It was something she never would have believed if she hadn't seen it herself. During the past few months Joanne had run all over the county auditioning bands, checking out caterers, investigating new sources for supplies, supervising the fundraising activities. She even had got Benji into the act, running programs on the school computer to determine the best way of using the prom funds. Yet as far as Barbara could tell, she still had the time to keep up her schoolwork and be friendly to just about everyone at school. The only thing that seemed to have suffered was her relationship with Brian, who was getting pretty jealous about the amount of time she was spending away from him. Before, Barbara had considered Joanne phony and insincere. Now she realized she had been the insincere one, making snap judgments about things she hadn't understood.

And now one of her judgments could get most of the school mad at her.

She turned her attention to the manila folder Mr. Goffit had given her. She couldn't believe the way the school board members had twisted her editorial to make it appear she supported them. She didn't have to read all the way through to realize there was nothing in there she could support. Yet what could she do? Frustrated, she flung the report up in the air, scattering the crisp white pages around the room.

Barbara caught up with Miss Gregg after school that day. "Do you have a few minutes?" she asked. "I've got to talk to you."

"Meet me at the *Call* office in five minutes," Miss Gregg replied, concerned. "I've got to bring these reports over to the faculty office."

For the second time that day Barbara sat down at her desk, feeling the consequences of having the power of being able to speak her mind on the pages of the newspaper.

"What can I do for you?" Miss Gregg asked as she walked breezily into the room. She flung her attaché case on the side counter and pulled up a stool next to the desk.

"Miss Gregg, I'm in trouble!"

"What's wrong?" she asked, alarmed.

"The school board wants me to help them kick the clubs out of the school."

"Why?"

"Because of this." Barbara handed her the old editorial. "They said I inspired them to take the action. I'm so ashamed of myself."

Miss Gregg scanned the page. "I could see why they felt you were an ally. What's the problem?"

"I never should have written it. It was stupid, and I don't believe most of it anymore."

"What changed your mind?"

"I thought the clubs were unfair the way they made some kids feel left out. I still don't approve of them totally, but I see now that they have a good side—like the way they've organized the prom, for instance."

Miss Gregg nodded. "It's too bad that you made such a strong statement in print. We all do things we later regret. But you have an important responsibility as editor of this newspaper. You're an opinion maker, and what you print has an important influence on readers—whoever they may be."

Barbara was taken aback by Miss Gregg's comments. She had never expected her to react like this. "There are some people around here who think nobody cares about what I have to say."

"Obviously someone does—or we wouldn't be here now."

"Yeah, the wrong people," Barbara mumbled.

Miss Gregg looked at her sympathetically. "I'm so sorry that I sound as if I'm riding you. But you're very talented, and this is one of the problems you're going to have to deal with if you decide to make journalism your career."

"I guess you're right," Barbara said. "But it doesn't solve my problem."

"Okay, here are the facts. You wrote an

editorial critical of something that goes on at school. Some school board members read it, jumped to their own conclusions, and took your suggestion one step beyond. You're against their proposal—and you still have a platform from which to speak. What do you think you do?"

"Write another editorial," she answered. "I plan to do that. But I have a feeling that's not going to be enough."

"Have you spoken to the club presidents about this?"

"Not yet—I've been too embarrassed."

"Don't you think it's time you swallowed your pride? It would certainly help your cause if you all worked together on this."

"I guess you're right. We could circulate petitions, make our own speeches to the board," she said, sounding more enthusiastic.

"That's the spirit," Miss Gregg said, smiling. Hearing a knock on the door, she turned around.

"There you are, Jacki." Mr. Rozzo poked his head inside. "Don't mean to interrupt—"

Miss Gregg smiled warmly at the economics teacher. "We're almost through, Matt."

"Fine. I'll meet you out at my car." Then, turning his attention to Barbara, he said, "Missed you in class today. Naughty. Naughty." He wagged his finger at her in jest.

There was a time when Barbara would have been embarrassed at her teacher's comment and would have been defensive about it. But now she answered back in mock defiance, "Hey, Mr. Rozzo, even I have to take some time off every now and then."

He smiled. "See you tomorrow." He closed the door behind him as he left.

Barbara was blushing slightly as she said to Miss Gregg, "You like Mr. Rozzo, don't you?"

It was Miss Gregg's turn to blush. "Yes, I do. He's a very nice man—and funny, too."

"I've always had a crush on him," Barbara kidded.

"That's sweet. I hope you don't mind my asking, but is there a special boy in your life, Barbara?"

"There's a guy I'm kind of interested in," Barbara admitted after a pause. "But he can't stand me."

"Are you sure?" Miss Gregg said. "Does he know how you feel?"

"Probably not. Everytime I see him I end up fighting with him. But I can't stop thinking of him when he's not around. It's crazy, isn't it?"

"Not really."

"Oh, Miss Gregg, sometimes I just don't understand boys," Barbara moaned.

Miss Gregg got up and walked over to the window. "When it comes to boys, there are a few universal truths. When I was your age, for instance, I had a crush on a boy in my class. I used to stare at him—we had history together— but I never got up the nerve to speak to him in class. I always imagined that he would suddenly discover me and make the first move. I thought boys were supposed to make the first move anyway. Well, I never did anything about it and—you guessed it—he ended up dating someone else. I found out much later on that he did like me but was afraid I'd reject him."

"That's too bad," Barbara said. "You must have really liked him."

Miss Gregg smiled wistfully. "I was a lot like you. I was under pressure at home to get good grades, and I was kind of shy around boys. I also didn't know how to juggle the two. I was afraid that if I spent too much time on one, I'd lose the other."

"So what did you do?" Barbara asked.

"Well, missing out on that one boy taught me that there was more to life than grades, grades, grades. And I also realized that sometimes a girl has to take the first step with a guy."

Barbara was surprised by the intensity with which Miss Gregg spoke. "So I should make an effort to work things out with this boy?"

"What do you have to lose? The worst thing that could happen is that he still won't like you. If that's so, then you'll have a good cry and then be ready to put him in your past and get on with the rest of your life."

"That's exactly what Kris said. You both make it sound so easy."

"You're a good kid, Barbara. I want to see you happy. Besides," she added mysteriously, "I have a feeling this boy might not be as hostile as you think."

"Miss Gregg," Barbara said firmly, "do you know something I don't know?"

"All I know is what I see around school," she answered cryptically. "And if this boy is who I think he is—I think you've got a fighting chance."

"What do I do?"

"Be his friend—and see what happens."

"I'll try."

"And remember, nothing happens overnight. Give yourself some time," she said. "And if you need to talk some more, I'll be here."

"Thanks," Barbara said.

Miss Gregg clasped her hand and smiled. "If you'll excuse me now, I have someone waiting for me."

Chapter 11

Barbara closed the door behind Miss Gregg then returned to her chair. It was all so confusing, she thought, reflecting on what both Kris and Miss Gregg had told her. But some things were becoming clearer to her now. She realized that the false, toughened attitude she had sometimes assumed with Michael had been her way of protecting herself so he couldn't hurt her. And that attitude, that layer of contempt Kris had spoken about, had kept Michael from discovering the real person. She had to try to break it down. If he didn't want to have anything to do with her, she had to know now, while there was still time to do something about it. She didn't want to end her senior year without giving herself—and Michael—a chance together.

But first there was the matter of the school board to settle. Sitting down before the old creaky typewriter in the *Call* office, she cranked out the editorial she was going to run in the upcoming issue.

* * *

In this column a few months ago I launched a tirade against the practice of pledging. Recent events have forced me to look back on that editorial with a certain amount of regret. I was wrong to have written so hastily about this practice without giving it the careful reflection it deserved. While it is true that I have had no desire to take part in the pledging ritual, it was unfair of me to have called on others to stop, simply because of my feelings.

But enough apologizing. The reason I'm writing this now is to call your attention to the proposal now before our school board, a proposal to ban these clubs from our school campus. I believe this proposal is unfair to the members of these clubs, and I urge everyone at Clear Lake, whether a club member or not, to join me in vigorous protest against this measure. The people who have conceived it are as unseeing and uncaring as I was when I wrote that earlier editorial. They fail to see the good these students can do, both in the goodwill they generate in school and the good deeds they perform in our community. Instead of condemning them, the board should be commending them for carrying on the fine tradition of community service and caring, from class to class, generation to generation. These clubs have been part of the fabric of Clear Lake since this school was founded thirty years ago. They should not be allowed to founder on the prejudice of a few narrow-minded citizens of the community.

If you care—as you should—please sign the petitions circulating around school, and join me at the school board meeting this Wednesday night.

The board may want to expel me, Barbara thought, after she had finished marking up the piece for the typesetter. She had never even come close to attacking the school board or any of its members on the editorial page before, but now she was willing to face whatever criticism they might lodge at her.

In a way, what she had to do next was even harder for her than writing the editorial. That evening she called Joanne and asked her to meet her before homeroom the next morning.

"What for?" Joanne asked.

"What I have to tell you has to be said in person," Barbara answered mysteriously. "I can't talk now, but believe me it's important. Will you meet me?"

"I guess so," Joanne said.

Barbara then called up Jason Jackson, Lance Rose, Brenda Syles, and Julie Pregerson, the presidents of the other clubs, and asked them to join her, too.

As Barbara rounded the corner to her locker the next morning, she found all five of them waiting expectantly for her.

"What's up, Vreeland?" Jason asked.

"I gather none of you are aware of the school board meeting next week," she began.

They looked at each other, shaking their heads.

"I thought so," she said. "The board was bound to stack the deck against you."

"You're not making any sense," Joanne interjected.

"It's kind of hard for me to say what I've got to say. You're not going to like it."

They looked at her expectantly, and Barbara took a deep breath, then began. "Yesterday I was approached by three members of the school board. They're going to introduce a measure at next week's meeting to ban your clubs from the school grounds."

"They can't do that," Brenda cried.

"Unfortunately, they can, and they will."

"What's your part in this, Vreeland?" Jason asked.

Joanne answered for her. "Isn't it obvious? It's all her idea."

"No, Joanne, it isn't. I'll admit they got the idea from that stupid editorial I wrote, but I'm just as upset about this as you are."

"Really?" Joanne shot back, unconvinced. "It's a little late for apologies. And I was just beginning to think you were all right."

"I'm sorry this happened."

"You ought to be. It's your fault."

"Hold it," Barbara stopped her. "You're not

saying anything I haven't already thought myself. But I'm on your side now."

"Look, this isn't going to affect me, I'll be graduating, but it's not fair to the rest of my girls," Joanne said. "How could you have done this?"

"I agree with you," Barbara cried. "I was dead wrong about you guys before, but I'm not going to let them kick your groups out of school for anything. I'm willing to fight. Are you?"

The club leaders looked at each other for a moment. "What do you have in mind?" Brenda asked.

"If we make out petitions and get signatures from most of the students and teachers, I think we can stop this thing. They were hoping to ram it through without giving you too much time to organize. I admit we still don't have too much time, but I think we can pull it off. I've written an editorial that'll be in the *Call* on Monday. The meeting is Wednesday night. We can stop them."

"I believe you mean it," Jason said, surprised.

"You'd better," Barbara said without missing a beat. "If any of you can think of anyone from the community who'll come out to support you, it'll really help."

"I think I could get Dr. Bardhoff from the hospital," Joanne ventured aloud.

"That's a start."

"We could probably get Coach Rogers, too," Brenda said.

"They're not going to get away with this," Barbara said excitedly. She looked meaningfully at Joanne, and she thought she could see the coldness begin to fade from her eyes.

"Let's go," Joanne said. "We'll talk later, Barb."

"Sure thing," Barbara said, smiling, before walking off to her homeroom.

Chapter 12

"There's hope for you yet."

Michael handed Barbara's typewritten copy of her editorial back to her. "I'm proud of you."

"Thanks." Barbara blushed slightly. "But the battle's not over yet."

"I'd never have believed it. You've got a heart after all," John chided from his familiar seat at the back of the room.

"C'mon, John, give her a break," pleaded Kris. "She admitted she was wrong."

"Yeah, leave her alone," Bobby said.

The *Call* staff was putting together the final touches on the April issue. Barbara had been pleased with its progress. As far as she was concerned, it was their best issue yet. Not the least of which was Michael's life management article, which she had decided to run on the front page. As she had suspected, he had been surprised when she told him she would print the article with minimal changes. But he was absolutely stunned when she praised him and told him it was the best thing he'd ever written.

"Who'll be at the meeting?" Michael asked.

"Right now, me and the five club presidents."

"What about the teachers?"

"It's not definite yet, but I think Coach Rogers and Mr. Tashmanski from the faculty association."

"I wish I could come," he said.

"You're welcome to," Barbara said sincerely. "We need club members who could make a good impression on those stiffs."

"C'mon, Barb, I'm not exactly the all-American boy."

"Maybe not," she smiled, "but you're the closest thing we have for now."

Michael chuckled and shot a skeptical glance at her, then dropped his lanky frame on the counter. "I wish I could, but my dad needs me at the warehouse."

"Anything the matter?"

"I don't want to talk about it now," he said quietly.

Barbara picked up his uneasiness. "I promise to come back with a full report, okay?"

"Okay." He smiled weakly.

The meeting was way beyond Barbara's expectations. She and Joanne and the others sat on folding chairs in front of the ten-member board, waiting patiently for their chance to speak.

After Mr. Goffit had finished a fifteen-minute introduction of his proposal, he recognized Barbara from the floor and invited her to speak. Barbara couldn't help but notice his smug-looking face, but she took a big deep breath and began her speech. Appealing to the board members she didn't know, she began by reading out of the manila folder Mr. Goffit had given her. But halfway through the first paragraph, she put down the folder and told the rest of the board where she had got it from and why. Then she introduced the rest of her new-found student friends and sat down as they eloquently defended themselves before the board.

In the end, the board defeated the motion six to four. Barbara was elated, of course, but her biggest victory that night came when the others invited her to come along for a celebration party at Emilio's. They took one of the round tables at the back of the restaurant and began the celebration with a toast to the board.

Then Joanne raised her soda and said, "To Barbara, without whose help we never would have made it."

"Thanks," Barbara said, "but you guys did all the work."

"It took courage to do what you did. I appreciate it," Joanne said. She clasped Barbara's shoulder in a gesture of friendship.

Chapter 13

The next day Barbara kept her word and gave Michael a full report on the meeting. After she had finished, she happened to mention that she was going into the city that afternoon to order some of the prom supplies, one of the chores he had assigned her to do weeks before. She was surprised when he asked if he could come along, but she agreed without question.

Ten minutes after school let out that afternoon, Barbara stood impatiently by her car in the school parking lot, waiting for Michael to show up. The April sky was unusually dark, and Barbara was sorry she hadn't brought along her rain jacket. It looked as if a downpour might start any minute.

Five minutes later Barbara began to wonder if Michael was having second thoughts. She hoped he didn't consider this trip a big inconvenience. She did everything she could to prevent herself from getting mad at him for being late. Somehow five minutes of repeating to herself "I'm not going to get mad" worked, for by the time Michael bounded across the black asphalt lot, his Ravens jacket trailing behind him in the wind, she was truly glad to see him.

"Sorry I'm late," he said as he opened the passenger door.

"It's okay," she said pleasantly. "We've got plenty of time." She slipped into her seat and started the ignition.

"Aren't you going to ask what kept me?"

"Should I?"

"Why not?"

Barbara shifted into first and then looked straight at Michael. "Okay. What kept you?"

"I had to talk to Mr. Leon."

Barbara couldn't figure out why Michael was making such a big deal about his speaking to the history teacher. "I suppose it was absolutely essential to talk over the causes of World War One?" She knew she was teasing him, but she felt he was asking for it.

"No, it had nothing to do with history. He went to Berkeley, and he's promised to tell me everything I need to know about it."

"So you've made up your mind to go there?" Barbara couldn't help but be pleased.

"Yep. I haven't been accepted yet, but I think I'll get in." He laughed. "I thought you'd want to know."

"I'm glad. But what changed your mind? I thought you were going to Cal State and surf every afternoon."

"I got to thinking that if I don't shape up, I'm in for lots of trouble."

"What happened to your life in plumbing? I thought it was going to lead you to a life of Porsches and blonds and beach houses."

"I'm not sure anymore. Dad's had some trouble lately, and I've had to come in and help out. Now that I see what it's really like, I'm not so sure I want to go into the business."

"What will you do?"

"I don't know. But I'll have a better chance of finding out if I go to Berkeley."

"There's hope for you yet," Barbara said, approaching the entrance to the freeway.

"And what does that mean?"

"I've always had trouble picturing you surrounded by toilet seats."

Michael laughed at the image. "I think I have, too." Then looking at her he added, "I have to admit that you had a little to do with it, too."

"I did?" She tried not to let her voice betray her excitement.

Michael shifted in his seat. "You did. When we started this life management stuff, I didn't take it very seriously. Pretending to be married—and with a kid no less. I guess my attitude made it kind of hard on you. I mean, there you were taking this whole thing very seriously. And there I was, thinking that if I looked at life as one big joke, it would all be easy sailing."

Barbara was disappointed. She had hoped he had chosen Berkeley because she had been

115

accepted there. Still, she *had* influenced him, which made her feel good.

"You mean I'm not the humorless shrew you made me out to be?"

"I wouldn't go quite that far," he hedged. "But the end result was that it made me see that if I don't put some effort into making something of myself, I could turn into a beach bum."

"Oh, Michael, it sounds as if things are really going to work out for you," Barbara said encouragingly.

A short while later they arrived at the party supply company Barbara had found in one of her earlier searches. The white stucco building was so nondescript that the two of them drove past it twice before discovering the small sign over the metal door.

"Are you sure this is it?" Michael asked. "It looks like a dump."

"It says Premium Party Supplies, right?"

Opening the door, they discovered a fantasy world. Stacked along the expanse of shelves were colorful streamers, party hats, favors, and a variety of decorations for any type of party. On the floor were tables, chairs, sculptures, and screens of every size.

A tall, heavyset man approached them. "What can I do for you kids?"

"We're from Clear Lake High," Barbara said. "I called earlier."

"Oh, yeah," he said. "Come this way."

The man, whose name tag said Sid, led them into a room to the left of the big room they had entered. "We usually get a lot of orders for this stuff around Valentine's Day," he remarked.

Inside were hearts and artificial flowers of every kind and color. Pink hearts made out of satin, red paper hearts the size of billboards, neon hearts, electric hearts, and even a few old Day-glo hearts. Lined up against one wall were rows upon rows of artifical roses in pink, white, red, purple, and yellow.

"Wow," said Michael, "I've never seen anything like this before."

"Look here," Barbara said, walking toward the back of the room. Stacked along this wall were little Cupid statues. "They're just like Kevin's, don't you think?"

"Uh-huh."

"Kinda cute, huh?"

'I never thought I'd hear you say that," he remarked.

She smiled innocently.

During the next twenty minutes they continued to rummage through the supplies. After deciding most of the hearts were inappropriate, they returned to the main room. As they walked along the aisles, picking out streamers and fold-out balls, and other supplies they felt would go with the prom decor, Sid followed behind them, checking off each item on a giant master list.

"We'll be able to have these in time for our prom?" she asked.

"No problem," Sid answered. "We'll even deliver them if you like."

"Wonderful," she said. "Michael, you ready to go?"

Michael was off in the other room, holding a small red satin heart in his hand. He held it up for just a second, as if thinking of something, then tossed it back into the bin it had come from. "Sure, coming," he said, catching up with her as she walked toward the exit.

Opening the door, Barbara and Michael discovered a downpour in progress. Although it was only four-thirty, the sky was dark gray. There was no letup in sight.

"We're going to have to make a run for it," Barbara said glumly.

"Do you have an umbrella in the car? I can get it," Michael said.

"No."

"You mean 'Barbara the Organized' wasn't prepared for this?"

"C'mon, Michael, I'm not perfect."

"Take my jacket," Michael offered.

"That's okay." Barbara shook her head. "It's not that far." She retrieved her keys from her bag and ran outside before Michael could get her to change her mind. He followed behind.

Nevertheless, Barbara was soaked by the time she reached the car. "This is what I get for wearing a T-shirt today."

"You should have taken my jacket."

"You're just as soaked as I am, so what

difference would it make? I'll run the heater for a few minutes to get off the chill."

But when she started the engine and flicked the heat switch, nothing but cold air came pouring out. "Darn it," she complained. "I thought I'd fixed it."

"*You'd* fixed it?"

"Yeah, I put in a new fuse a couple of months ago, but I guess something went wrong."

Michael shook his head. "I've never known a girl like you."

"Thanks, I take it as a compliment."

"You should." Michael stared ahead at the traffic. They were coming to the approach to the San Diego Freeway, and they both could see that the road was already clogged with rush-hour traffic.

"Looks like we're going to be on the parking lot for a while," Barbara said, switching on the radio. Everyone on the freeway had their lights on, and from her vantage point Barbara could see an endless ribbon of taillights that reminded her of the decorations in the Valentine's Day room.

"Turn here," Michael said suddenly, pointing to the upcoming intersection.

"Turn where?"

"Make a right turn at the light. I know a way to avoid the freeway."

"But it's thirty miles to Clear Lake. The side streets will take forever."

"It's better than being stuck in five lanes of bumper-to-bumper traffic. Trust me."

"Okay," she said skeptically. She edged the little car over to the right lane. "I hope you know your way around here, 'cause I don't."

"Don't worry, I'll have us back in Clear Lake in no time."

Michael expertly navigated Barbara through the streets of West Los Angeles as they slowly made their way back to the northern edge of the San Fernando Valley. The small stucco bungalows they passed gradually gave way to larger, lavishly landscaped houses as they approached the Santa Monica Mountains. The steady rain kept the visibility low, and Barbara had to ease off the gas pedal a bit as they ventured into the misty and winding road up the mountains. It never failed to amaze Barbara that all this virgin land, interrupted here and there by a housing development or two, was stuck right in the middle of Los Angeles. But she wasn't really thinking about that now—all her thoughts were on the boy sitting next to her.

"You're pretty quiet," he said, turning the volume down on an old Led Zeppelin song.

"I'm concentrating on driving. It's miserable," she said.

"Want me to take over?"

"I can handle it," she assured him.

"Why do you have to do everything for yourself?"

Barbara heard the mildly complaining tone

120

in his voice. Ordinarily her next comment would have been something like "What's the matter, haven't you ever seen a girl with brains?" or something to that effect, and the next thing she knew she'd be in the middle of another clash of wills with him. Catching herself, she decided to take another approach. "I just meant that I was doing all right. But if you want to drive, I'll let you."

"You really mean it?"

"Sure." In that moment she pulled off to the shoulder and shifted into neutral. "It's all yours."

Michael smiled and said, "It's okay. We'd have to get out of the car to change seats, and I don't want you to get wet again."

"Fine with me." She edged the car back onto the road.

"I think that's the first time in our lives you've ever offered to share something with me," he said.

"There's a first time for everything," she said lightly.

"No, Barbara, I'm serious. There *is* something different about you."

"What makes you think so?"

"I don't know exactly, but you always used to try and top everyone else. What's happened?"

"You."

"Me? What do I have to do with it?"

"You've shown me it's really true about all work and no play makes Barbara a dull girl."

"I have?"

"Well, I've done a lot of thinking lately, and, I don't know, but it seems as if I've been kind of hard on myself. I used to think it was mostly my father hassling me about my grades all the time—but I gave myself almost as much trouble as he did."

"How so?"

"Oh, you know, thinking I always had to get A's, trying to make things, and sometimes people, turn out exactly the way I wanted them to. But life's just not that perfect."

"Speaking of being less than perfect, there's the freeway again, and it looks just as jammed up as ever. I think we're going to have to stay on these roads all the way back."

"If you're not in a hurry, neither am I." Barbara was content to stay in this car with Michael for as long as he'd let her. For the first time since that day at Emilio's, they were talking to each other like two people who cared for each other.

The whishing rhythm of the wiper blades against the windshield was the only sound for the next few minutes as they each were wrapped up in thought. Michael was trying to figure out if this change in Barbara was for real or whether it was just another one of her plans to throw him off the track. For the past few months he had felt Barbara was teasing him, acting as if she liked him one minute and hated him the next. It bothered him because he thought he could really like her. He already thought she was special—not like Marcy or some of the other girls he knew. Barbara was the kind of girl who had a lot to offer a guy: she was smart and independent, but she also seemed to have a soft side that he'd like to know more about. But he wasn't willing to open up to her—not just yet anyway—until he received some kind of sign from her that she really felt something for him.

Was she doing that now? he wondered. He remembered that day in Emilio's when Barbara had seemed so carefree and animated, not at all like the person she was at the *Call* or in class. He had felt comfortable with her then and had been considering asking her out for more than a pizza when she suddenly had turned cold on him. After that she seemed to keep him at a distance, as if she were saying, "Don't come too close." So he hadn't. But he hadn't stopped thinking about her and wondering if she would ever let him near.

They were halfway through the valley now, passing by an endless procession of tract houses and shopping centers. The rain continued its steady downpour over the road in front of them. It hardly ever rained in this area, but when it did it was as if the heavens had decided to store up water and unleash it all at once. The road, slick with months' worth of oil and dirt, was as slippery as any ice-covered stretch of pavement, and as treacherous. At several points along the way, Barbara had to steer carefully to avoid going into a skid. She forced herself to concentrate completely on the road. That was fortunate because a few miles down the road, after she had driven over some debris, she heard something go "pop" on the left side of the car.

Gently she eased off the gas pedal and maneuvered the car out of the flow of traffic. "I think it's the tire," she said nervously to Michael. She sighed as she turned off the engine.

"Let me look. Do you have a flashlight?"

"It's in the glove compartment. I'll go out with you." She opened the door to her side, watching out for passing cars. But the traffic was light now in this residential district. Looking down she cursed silently at the left front tire, now squashed flat on the bottom.

"We must have hit something in the road," she said sullenly to Michael, who bent down next to her to inspect the tire.

"Where's your spare?"

"In the back. I'll get it," she said loudly, trying to make herself heard over the rain.

"Let me help. I'll jack up the car. Why don't you set out the flares? You have flares, don't you?"

Barbara nodded. "I can take care of the tire. Why don't you get back in the car? You're soaked."

Michael looked at her with a mixture of exasperation and admiration for her tenacity. "I could say the same for you, but I know better than to order you back in the car. Let's do it together, okay?"

Barbara smiled. "Okay. I'll get the flares."

As she did so she turned back to face Michael. Now hunched over the front of the car, his muscles working steadily to raise it off the ground, Barbara thought he looked like a man ready to take on the responsibilities of the world. She felt a yearning ache inside her. Even the sight of his rain-drenched hair, curling in flat tendrils against his neck, only added to his appeal.

She ran to his side just as he was about to take off the tire. "How's it going?"

"Fine. We'll be on the road any minute now," he said, loosening the lug nuts and placing them carefully in the upturned hubcap.

"Is there anything I can do?"

"You can keep me company," he said.

Barbara felt the meaning behind those words and smiled. At that moment there was nothing else she wanted to do but be there by his side. "Thanks for helping," she said.

"It's no big deal."

"I have a confession to make. I've never changed a tire before. I don't know if I could have done it by myself."

"Really?" Michael was surprised. Wiping away a wet strand of hair he added, "It's not that hard. Watch me—so you'll know for next time."

125

Michael placed the spare tire on the raised wheel. "Feels a little light," he said. "But I think we'll be able to make it back on it." Then he wound the nuts back on the wheel.

"See, Barb, now you take the wrench and turn it tight. Here, try this one." He handed her the wrench.

"Like this?" Barbara gave the wrench a little twist forward.

Michael placed his hands over hers to demonstrate how to use the tool. Even though they were as wet as the rest of him, Barbara could feel their warmth. He was huddled over her now, and the feelings coming over her were just as confusing and exciting as they had been the day they had danced in the *Call* office. We must look like a couple of waterlogged wrecks, she thought, but her looks didn't matter to her now. She no longer minded the rain either, which now felt more like a glorious spring shower. She wouldn't have minded staying out in it all night if it meant she could remain close to this boy, who made her feel so wonderful.

"There we are," he said triumphantly, placing the hubcap back on the wheel and lowering the jack. "Let's put this stuff back and get out of here."

When Michael came back from putting the jack away, he saw Barbara still standing in the rain, her bare arms dripping little drops onto her water-soaked shoes. "You must be freezing," he said sympathetically. Taking off his jacket he said, "You're going to wear this whether you like it or not."

Barbara was in no mood to argue. As he reached over to drape the jacket over her shoulders, she looked up at him, and in that second she saw the look of sympathy in his eyes. But she didn't want his sympathy, she wanted his love. Tears began to form in her eyes, and within a few seconds she was weeping openly, embarrassed by her display of emotion but powerless to stop it.

"Hey, don't cry," he said. "Everything's fine now." He held her close, placing his hand on the back of her neck and rubbing gently.

"I don't know wh—why I'm—crying," she said between sobs.

"It's okay," he said, whispering in her ear.

But the feelings overwhelming her were too sudden and too scary to understand. She broke away from his grasp, feeling a strange kind of relief that she wasn't in his arms.

"We've got to get back," she said coldly.

"Whatever you say," Michael said flatly, more confused by her actions than ever.

"Please, let's go." Hastily she opened the door and started up the engine. Michael followed her inside.

"Barbara, I—"

"I don't want to talk about it. I'm sorry," she said, convinced that Michael now saw her as some kind of idiot. She didn't want him to rub it in. Wordlessly they drove back to Clear Lake, and ten minutes later Barbara pulled up to his house.

Michael wanted to say something to her, but Barbara turned away, indicating she didn't want to talk anymore. Without another word he got out of the car and slammed the door shut.

"I've really blown it now," she said sadly to herself.

Chapter 14

It was close to seven when Barbara walked into her house. Still dripping wet, she entered through the garage and removed her grimy, soaked flats in the laundry room. They're probably ruined, she said to herself in passing—just one more thing ruined by her foolish behavior.

She was still wearing Michael's jacket; in her hurt and confusion she had forgotten to give it back to him. She took it off now and placed it on the dryer, a small puddle quickly forming underneath it.

"Barbara, what happened?" her mother called, hurrying into the room. "My dear, you're a mess."

"I know, Mom," she said sullenly. She didn't feel like volunteering any more information.

But her mother quickly spotted the jacket on the dryer. Picking it up, she saw the rope-lettered name on the jacket front. "Whose is this?" she demanded. "Have you been out with someone?"

"What if I have?" she said, not caring.

"Barbara, what's gotten into you? Last week you were partying with Kris. Now out with a boy without telling us. You know the rules."

"Gee, Mom, isn't that a joke. How many times have I been anywhere with a boy during the week?"

"I don't recall—"

"That's because the answer is none," she cried. "And it still is. Michael McNally and I went looking at prom stuff, that's all." New tears of anger began forming in her eyes.

"That's no excuse for being late for dinner." Her father's voice now filled the small room.

"And who is this Michael? . . . Oh, I remember now," her mother said. "Isn't he the nice little boy you used to do school projects with?"

"How long have you been seeing this boy? Why haven't you told us?" her father demanded.

"I'm not seeing him!" Barbara shouted, wishing her parents could see how upset she was. "I'll probably never see him again." She ran away, wanting nothing more right now than the peace and quiet of her room. Her father started to go after her, but she heard her mother tell him, "It's better if you leave her alone for now."

By the next morning Barbara had composed herself, and she had come up with a few conclusions about the incident with Michael. She had let fear get in the way of her feelings for him. She knew that she wanted—no, needed—him now. Yet when she thought about telling him how she felt, she panicked; she didn't know how to handle these new emotions.

So she resolved once again to keep her feelings to herself. She would still try to be pleasant and friendly to him, of course, and hope that he, too, would still take an interest in her. But if he didn't—well, that was something she'd have to deal with later.

Life management class the next day, however, was almost unbearable for her. Still embarrassed by her behavior, she looked down when Michael said hello to her. Fortunately for her Mr. Rozzo gave a lecture, so she didn't have to sit next to Michael or talk to him. Relieved when the bell rang, signaling the end of class, she raced out before he had a chance to say anything to her.

"Barbara, wait up!"

She turned around as quickly as she could in the crowded hall, surprised to see Kris, who ran to catch up with her. "Barb, I've got the greatest news!" she said, about to burst.

Making an effort to sound happy, Barbara said, "Tell me. But hurry, I've got to run to physics."

"Physics can wait, this can't. Mark has asked me to the prom!"

"That's super," Barbara said sincerely. "When did this happen?"

"Yesterday. I tried to reach you last night, but your mom said you'd gone to bed early."

"Yeah, I wasn't feeling too hot."

"Listen," Kris said, "I've got to get a dress. You busy after school?"

"You don't waste a minute, do you?" Barbara said as the warning bell rang. "Sure, I'll come."

"Meet you at the parking lot," Kris called, running backward down the hall.

"What do you think of this?" Kris said as she came out of the dressing room of the third boutique they had visited. She was wearing a dark blue gown with long sleeves and a V-neck.

"Not you." Barbara shook her head. "Not flashy enough."

"I thought so. But Mark says blue is his favorite color. I've got to find something in blue!"

"Relax, we've just started. Let's go back to the rack and take another look."

They walked down the soft, pink-carpeted floor to the party dresses section. Kris inspected the remaining four blue dresses on the size seven rack, rejecting three of them as being "not right," "too gross," and "not my style" in that order. But the last dress, a blue and white sheath with a low back, intrigued her.

Coming out of the dressing room a few minutes later, she asked, "Well?"

"I love it," Barbara said.

"I don't know," Kris wondered. "It doesn't seem to fit me right in here," she said, indicating her chest. "Why don't you try it on?"

"Me? What for? We've been over this, Kris. I'm not going."

"You are going," Kris corrected her. "I'm going to see to it."

"I've blown it with Michael," Barbara said.

"He's a dead issue," Kris said. "We'll find you someone else. Can't you think of anyone you'd like to go with?"

"Who? The prom is three weeks away, and all the neat boys are taken—although I have a feeling Brian Adams might be available soon."

Kris's eyes widened. "You mean Joanne's not going with him?"

"I'm not sure, but from the way she was acting the other night, I have a feeling she's had it with him. But even if she does break up with him, I can think of half a dozen P.K.'s who'd line up to get first crack at him."

"Maybe you'd have a shot at him, too," Kris said eagerly.

"No, he's not my type."

Kris paced the entranceway to the dressing room, trying to think of some other boys. "What about Bobby?"

"You've got to be kidding! Yech!"

"Okay, he's not Prince Charming. But he's a date. C'mon, Barb, you're not going to tell me you put all that work into the prom and aren't going to go."

"But Bobby?"

133

"You don't have to make up your mind now. Think about it. In the meantime, I want to see how you look in this dress."

"All right," Barbara said, more to keep Kris quiet than anything else. She followed her friend into the dressing room and watched her take off the dress. Dutifully she took off her clothes and put on the dress. Stepping back a little, she looked at herself in the three-way mirror with surprised pleasure. It fit perfectly, emphasizing her breasts and trim figure. Even the length was perfect. The dress made her look older, more sophisticated and—she noticed with a start—sexy. That thought made her giggle.

"I knew it was you," Kris said admiringly. "Buy it."

"That's ridiculous," Barbara said.

"Buy it before someone else does. You're going to the prom."

"Forget it. I don't even have a date yet. Nice try." With that she took off the garment and placed it neatly back on the hanger.

"You're going to be sorry," Kris warned.

Chapter 15

During the next few weeks Barbara saw her relationship with Michael as a marriage partner improve a little, as she continued her efforts to be more conciliatory. But she felt that the spark that had been ignited that evening in the rain had been extinguished for good. Although Michael was pleasant to her, he seemed to hold back any other feelings he might have had. She longed for the chance to express her feelings for him, but every time she tried, the picture of her crying popped into her head, and she retreated. She didn't want a repeat of that scene.

It was now the last week of May, and in just two days the prom would be a cherished memory. To those who went, that is. Barbara still didn't have a date. As she had threatened, Joanne did break up with Brian, shocking practically the entire school in the process. But even if Barbara had seriously thought about asking Brian, she couldn't. By the time she'd heard the news, Brian had already lined up a date with one of Joanne's sorority sisters.

The activity on the *Call* was slowing down. There would be one more issue out the second week of June, with graduation and senior prom news, year-end reviews, and final sports wrap-ups.

Barbara felt sad to be ending her work on the newspaper. She had written about her feelings in the May editorial: she had described the triumphs, the problems, the responsibilities, and the benefits that went along with her job. Now the responsibility for running the paper would be going to Bobby, who would officially be designated editor for next year at the end-of-the-year party that was being held that night.

Bobby, in fact, had made all the arrangements for the party, reserving the banquet room at the Florentine Palace, supervising the menu, and collecting the funds. Barbara could see he would carry on the tradition of the *Call.* But her admiration of him stopped there—as a prom date he just wouldn't do. Kris hadn't stopped lobbying for him—she wanted Barbara to participate in the prom festivities—but Barbara wouldn't budge. A part of her still fantasized about Michael.

Barbara was thinking about all this as she got ready for the party. She had her parents' permission to go, though it had taken a lot of discussion to get them to give in. Her parents admitted they might have been too strict with their rules, and they agreed that with just a few weeks of school left, Barbara owed it to herself to ease up on her studies. But they still wanted to know exactly where she was going—and with whom—when she went out.

She took her time getting ready, putting on a new sleeveless gauze dress and using more makeup than she normally wore. She brushed back her long hair until it shone, and then, satisfied she looked her best, she ran down the stairs and out to meet Kris by the car.

Miss Gregg and Mr. Rozzo were already at the restaurant when Kris and Barbara arrived. Bobby was there, too, anxiously counting heads, making sure everyone would show up.

"Barbara," he called when he spotted her. "You look great."

"Thanks, Bobby," she answered pleasantly. "Nice job you did," she added, glancing around the room.

"You mean it?" he said excitedly. "I didn't want to let you down."

"You couldn't do that," she answered, walking off to see who else was there. Bobby stood there beaming.

Barbara was speaking to Amy Newman, the *Call's* business manager, when she heard Michael's voice behind her. Involuntarily she shivered. How could she stand to spend the whole evening in the same room with him?

Leaving Amy, she took a cup of punch from the long table set up with drinks and hors d'oeuvres, then sat down at the banquet table, alone, while the rest of the staff mingled about. She could see Kris laughing about something with Bobby and wondered if she was putting him up to something. As a junior Bobby really couldn't ask her outright, but knowing Kris, Barbara didn't put it past her to think of a way to circumvent the rules.

Barbara was unusually quiet during dinner and barely touched her veal parmigiana. She felt Michael's eyes on her several times, and it made her uneasy.

After dinner she got up and made a little speech, thanking the staff for their work throughout the year. Then she announced the staff for the following year, ending with the official designation of Bobby as the new editor. She presented him with a little gift—a straw hat with a Press sign. To everyone's delight he immediately put it on, and in his acceptance speech he praised Barbara for all the help she had given him. To her surprise the rest of the staff applauded warmly. "The unsung hero," Amy called her. Barbara was deeply moved; she hadn't realized she had made such an impression on everyone. Even John was clapping vigorously, she noted.

The party began to break up soon afterward. Barbara was about to leave when Michael caught up with her and motioned her to a table near the door.

"I couldn't let you leave without adding my own appreciation of your work."

"Don't think you have to because everybody else did."

"I'm not like that. I really mean it."

"Thanks."

"Hey." He lifted up her chin with his fingers. "We're friends now, right?"

"Sure, friends," she repeated, wishing it could be more.

Mr. Rozzo, spotting them, walked over to their table. "Am I interrupting?"

"You are, but it's okay," Michael said.

"You don't know how glad I am you've worked out your problems in class. I was worried about you two."

"Everything's under control," Barbara said. She was sorry Mr. Rozzo had taken this moment to talk. She had been hoping to find out if Michael had another reason for coming up to her right then.

"Yeah, we found out we could get a lot more done by talking instead of fighting," Michael added.

"I hope you've learned something," Mr. Rozzo said, becoming serious for a moment. "What you read in a book can't begin to teach you how to make it in the real world the way experience can. I wish they had had a course like this when I was in school."

"We learned we had to learn how to get

along with each other to make it through your course," Michael said, putting his arm around the back of Barbara's chair. "But," he added, joking, "now that we're almost through, I can go back to hating her."

But Barbara wasn't amused, she was furious. "So that's all I've been?" she said angrily, rising from her chair. "Just someone you had to get along with so you'd pass a course?" She ran out of the restaurant, slamming the door behind her.

"Barbara, wait," Michael said, running after her. But by the time he got outside she was already in her car, heading for home.

Chapter 16

"What's your problem, Vreeland?"

Barbara ignored Michael's question as she took her seat in economics. She hoped Mr. Rozzo would walk into the room right now so she wouldn't have to face the boy who was making her feel so confused.

"Barbara, I want an anwser. Why are you ignoring me?" He followed her to her seat, crouching so his face was even with hers.

"I'm not ignoring you. I just wanted to sit down. I'm tired," she said.

"You're not a very good liar," he said.

"Quiet, everyone will hear," she whispered.

"Let them," he said adamantly. "Tell the whole world why you're ignoring me."

"I don't like it when someone greets me by saying 'what's your problem'—like there's something wrong with me."

Michael rolled his eyes. "I'm sorry, but when a girl walks out on a guy and says things that hurt him, he wants to know why."

She looked at him strangely. "Hurt you? I—"

"Okay, people, let's get to our seats." Mr. Rozzo walked briskly through the door, setting his books on his desk.

"We've got to talk," Michael said, making his way to his seat.

Mr. Rozzo spent the entire period continuing his discussion of income tax forms. Barbara tried to concentrate on the pros and cons of itemizing deductions, hoping that it would help her erase Michael's last comments from her mind. But it didn't work. What had she done? she wondered. She thought of sending him a note but dismissed the idea, worried that Mr. Rozzo would catch her. She wondered if Michael was looking at her now, if he was wondering what she was thinking. She was afraid to turn around and see.

After class Michael walked up to her. "Come with me," he said.

"Where to?"

"Where nobody will bother us."

Michael strode purposefully out of the room, down the long green corridor. Barbara practically had to run to keep up with him, and it didn't take long for her to realize where Michael was heading—to the *Call* office. He obviously intended to say more than a few words to her.

Inside the newspaper office, he sat down in

Barbara's chair and motioned for her to sit on the counter by the windowsill.

"Give it to me straight," he began. "Why did you run out on me?"

Barbara looked up at him. He didn't seem angry at her, just confused.

"You made fun of me," she said.

"You've got to do better than that."

"How am I supposed to feel when you tell Mr. Rozzo you're just being nice to me because of the project?"

"I was joking!" he cried. "Couldn't you tell?"

"It's no joking matter when you like some—" She stopped herself, realizing she had at last revealed the secret she had been keeping in her heart.

A slow smile started to form on Michael's face, gradually revealing his dimples. Barbara thought he was going to laugh and really make her feel stupid. But all he did was say quietly, "You like me?"

"You don't understand." Barbara dropped her hands on her lap.

"So explain." He moved the chair closer to her.

Barbara rubbed the inside of her left eye, trying to wipe away the tear she felt beginning to form. "I don't know if I can," she said, sighing. "One minute there you were, the boy I had spent my entire school life bickering with. And then the next minute there I was, falling for you.

I kept telling myself for the longest time, 'You're crazy, Barbara. You're falling for a guy who doesn't even care about you.'"

"Oh, Barbara," Michael said, reaching for her hand. He squeezed it, and she grasped it strongly.

"Let me go on," she said. "I've gone this far—I might as well tell you everything...." Beginning with the day in the pizza parlor, through the night she had been terrified to be with him, Barbara told him everything that had been going through her mind.

"And then last night was the last straw. Hearing you say you didn't feel the same way about me hurt too much. I had to leave. I—"

"Barbara." Michael lifted her from the counter and embraced her. "You funny, sweet girl." Loosening his grip, he reached over and wiped away the tear that had finally managed to fall down Barbara's cheek.

Barbara managed a faint smile.

"That's better," he said, taking her hand again. "You don't know how happy I am to hear all that."

"You are?"

"I shouldn't have made that joke. But for the longest time I thought you didn't care about me. I thought you were just being nice to me the past couple of weeks because of the project. And it bothered me. You see, something happened to me last winter. I realized how much you've got going for you as a person and how much I wanted to be with you. But every time I got up enough nerve to ask you out, you'd start to act cold to me, as though you didn't like me at all. So I didn't say anything—I didn't know what else to do.

"But I also knew we'd be graduating soon, and if I didn't get into Berkeley, I might never see you again. So last night seemed like a good time. But that's when Mr. Rozzo came up to us and spoiled everything. I felt really weird, so I made a joke that ruined everything for you."

"But I *do* like you, Michael," Barbara said.

"We almost blew it. All those lectures about communication, and neither one of us could say how we really felt."

Barbara nodded ruefully.

"After all this, will you go out with me Sunday?"

"Yes," she answered happily, hugging him again.

"Great." Michael looked at his watch. "I've got some unfinished business to take care of right now. See you later tonight at the gym." He kissed her lightly on the nose.

"Oh, Barbara," he added, turning around at the door. "Sorry I made you cut class."

She smiled, motioning with her arms that it was no big deal. "It was worth it," she said under her breath.

Barbara decided to spend the rest of that period in the *Call* office, checking the progress of the final issue, tidying up her files, doing busywork. It was all she could do to keep from opening up the window wide and shouting at the top of her lungs, "He's mine! Michael McNally likes me!" But she contented herself with keeping the knowledge to herself for the time being. The world would know soon enough.

About ten minutes before the end of the period, Barbara remembered that it was Kris's lunch period and she hadn't told her friend the good news. On the other hand, she thought, if she hurried she'd be able to catch Kris before she left the cafeteria. How good it would feel to be the one talking about a boyfriend for a change. The word sounded so sweet to her ears. He *is* my boyfriend now, she thought, her heart caressing the word.

The Clear Lake cafeteria was located in the center of the school, adjacent to the auditorium. Barbara usually went in the east entrance, the one closest to her physics class, but because the west entrance was the one closest to the *Call* office, that was the one she walked through now. Flinging open the door to the massive room, she spotted a couple, their backs to her, huddled close together at a nearby table. The boy had his arm around the girl, and her face was buried in his shoulder. The boy had black curly hair and the girl long red hair. There was no mistaking who it was: Michael and Marcy Mitchell.

Unable to bear the sight, Barbara spun around and ran out of the cafeteria and back to the sanctuary of the *Call* office.

Chapter 17

"We're going to be late," Kris cried as she walked into Barbara's bedroom later that evening. "Hey, what's wrong?"

Barbara was hunched over her desk, moping. She had been sitting there since she had come home from school. "I'm not going."

Kris couldn't believe Barbara was dropping out of setting up for the prom at this late date.

"Joanne wants us there at seven, and it's ten to already." She flung her bag over her shoulder as a signal to go. "What's your problem?"

"Leave me alone," she said, her back still turned to Kris.

"Don't tell me you're upset 'cause you don't have a date. I told you—"

"No," she said, turning around. "It's worse."

Kris threw her bag on the bed and sat down at the edge, careful not to mess up the quilt. "Do you want to talk?"

"I'm so miserable." Barbara then told Kris

about her conversation with Michael and how her short-lived happiness was shattered.

"He was holding her so close—like I didn't even exist."

"I didn't see anything. Are you sure it was them?"

"Positive," she said as she got up and moved over to the window seat.

"And you didn't say anything to him?"

"What could I say? I should have known he'd turn out to be a—"

"Whoa." Kris stopped her. "It just doesn't make any sense. Why would he go out of his way to tell you he cares for you if he's got something going with Marcy?"

"Maybe all he wants is to collect names for his little black book!" she spat out.

"Michael's not like that—and you know it."

"He *is* taking her to the prom," she said, wringing her yarn doll in her hands.

"He made that date ages ago."

"He could have broken it."

"Maybe he didn't want to hurt her."

"So he hurt me? Great," she said sarcastically, tossing the doll on the floor.

"Look, he'll be at the gym tonight. Why don't you ask him about it?"

"I can't do that!"

"You were able to talk to him earlier."

"Things are different now."

"Really?" The tone in Kris's voice surprised Barbara.

"Yes," Barbara said.

"Then do yourself a favor and get a date for the prom. Quick."

"I can't. It's too late."

"I know someone who's available." Kris rummaged through her bag and came up with her address book. Flipping through the pages, she found the number she was looking for and began to dial before Barbara realized what she was doing.

"Stop," Barbara wailed. "Kris, I—"

"You're lucky, Bobby's line is busy," Kris said, putting down the phone. "Let's go. We can call him from the gym."

Barbara glanced in the mirror, examining her bloodshot eyes. "Let me get myself together," she said. She dabbed some light green shadow on her eyes and mascara on her lashes, hoping it would make her look more alive. Then, with more enthusiasm than she felt, she said, "Let's go show that prom committee a thing or two."

"That's the spirit," Kris said, once again fumbling through her bag. "Want some gum?" she offered.

By the time they arrived at the high school, the gym had begun its metamorphosis from athletic court to romantic paradise. Brian and a couple of the wrestlers were already on tall ladders, stringing rows of multicolored streamers across the length of the high ceiling. Joanne stood across the room, supervising the construction crew which was building the platform for the band. In her hand was a legal pad filled with lists of things to do.

"I don't believe it," Kris said, noticing Joanne's ragged old jeans, uncharacteristic flannel shirt, and the bandanna covering her hair. "Did her mother cut off her clothing allowance?"

"Cut it out," Barbara said, walking toward the committee leader. "She's all right."

"I'm so glad you girls are here," Joanne gushed when she saw them. "My girls haven't shown yet," she added pointedly.

"We came to work," Barbara said.

Joanne thought for a moment, then scanned the sheets in front of her. "I think we'd better start with the wall murals. You two can handle a panel at a time, can't you?"

"Sure," Kris answered.

"You haven't seen Michael around anywhere, have you? He's supposed to be bringing in the palm trees."

Barbara shook her head. The room was beginning to fill up as more and more members of the committee filed in, but Michael was nowhere to be seen.

To Barbara's surprise that was the last she thought of him for the next hour, as she concentrated on setting up the murals. The whole room seemed to buzz with the anticipation of the prom now; it was an electric feeling that

Barbara found infectious. All together there were about thirty people there, each hard at work in some corner of the room, though she was sure that nobody considered what they were doing work. Someone had brought a radio, and the hard-driving rock music in the air added to the partylike atmosphere.

After a few false starts, Barbara and Kris attached the canvas panels to one wall and stepped back to admire their work.

"If I didn't know better, I'd swear I was looking at the ocean," Kris said.

"It's amazing. Kevin's a genius," Barbara agreed. "Look, you can even see the reflection of the moon in the water! It makes me wish I were going to be here," she said wistfully.

"You can," Kris insisted. "I've got Bobby's number with me."

After a moment's hesitation, Barbara took it. She was resigned at least to the thought of having Bobby as an escort. Dodging ladders and boxes of party decorations, she made her way out of the gym, toward a pay phone. The relative quiet of the hall unnerved her a little as she walked to the phone outside the principal's office.

She looked at the number in the address book for another minute, getting up her courage. "If I'm going to do it, I'd better do it now," she said at last, putting the dime in the slot and dialing. Her heart beat with nervousness as she waited for him to pick up at the other end. She hadn't even thought of what she was going to say to him.

Five rings. Ten rings. Fifteen rings. He's not there, she concluded, feeling a little odd. She had originally picked up the phone, hoping he wouldn't answer it, but now that he hadn't, she felt a wave of disappointment. Now she definitely wouldn't be going to the prom.

Slowly she walked back to the room. Standing by the gym entrance, taking it all in, she felt more alone than ever. Everywhere she looked there were kids laughing or dancing or sitting on the bleachers taking a break. The fringed, pink and lavender streamers were almost all in place. They helped to close in the room, to make it more intimate. Although the tables and chairs still had to be set up, Barbara could close her eyes and imagine how the room would look with everyone dressed in their gowns and tuxes. For a long time she had been able to convince herself that the prom was never to be a reality for her, so the prospect of not going hadn't really bothered her. But now that she had come so close to going, she realized just how much she would miss not being part of it.

She felt the best way to keep from falling to pieces was to get back to work with a vengeance. Noticing a box of foldout balls in one corner, she began to set them up. So what if nobody was ready to hang them yet? She had to do something—and right now she wanted to be alone.

Occasionally she would glance back to see if Michael had arrived. Although she tried to tell herself it didn't matter, she couldn't help but be concerned. It wasn't like him to shirk off a responsibility like this. As head of the decorating committee, he should have been here hours ago.

Fortunately Joanne had things under control, Barbara noticed. She even had Brian working, although he was noticeably cool to her. So were Denise and Lisa, she noticed. Joanne was still rather vague about her own prom plans. The rumor going around was that she'd be there with Benji, though nearly everyone was betting she would chicken out. Barbara was sort of hoping she would go with him though. Benji was a nice guy—if a bit strange for her tastes—and deserved to be there.

"Need any help?" came a voice from behind Barbara's left shoulder.

"Michael," she gasped, turning around to face him.

Standing there before her in his blue satin jacket, his hair windblown from being outside, he looked so handsome she was ready to melt. But then she remembered that scene in the cafeteria, and her face hardened.

"There was something I forgot to ask you this morning," he began, looking a little sheep-

155

ish. "I know it's kind of late, but will you go to the prom with me?"

He looked so hopeful, so expectant, that Barbara wanted to erase that scene from her mind. "I—I don't know," she said hesitatingly.

Michael pulled her close, his expression indicating he didn't understand her reluctance. "I wanted to ask you before, but I'd already asked Marcy, and I had to clear things up with her before I felt I could say anything to you."

"So that's what I saw," she gasped.

"You saw us—in the cafeteria? Oh, boy," he said, shaking his head. "You gotta let me explain. She got really upset. I had to hold her so the whole school wouldn't hear her crying. Then I felt so guilty I asked her out to dinner tonight, as sort of an apology. But you know what she did? After making me feel like a heel for dumping her, she casually mentions she was about to dump me so she could go to the prom with John. Can you believe it!"

Barbara grinned, relieved that her worst fears were unfounded. She looked over to where Michael was pointing, and sure enough there were Marcy and John hugging each other by the palm trees.

"Muscles," Michael muttered. "She says his muscles turn her on."

"She can have them—with my blessings," Barbara said, shyly raising her fingers to Michael's hair. "I've always had a thing for curly hair myself."

"So you'll go to the prom with me?"

"Yes," she said, hugging him.

Then Michael kissed her, a deep, searching kiss that Barbara responded to with all her heart. This time she wasn't afraid.

"Hey, people will notice," Michael said after a long moment.

"Let them," she responded.

They kissed again.

Chapter 18

Standing before her full-length mirror, Barbara smoothed down her satiny blue sheath dress. It was the same dress she had reluctantly tried on a few weeks back. Fortunately it was still on the rack when she had dashed to the boutique that morning.

Barbara had hardly slept that night. She got back from the gym around one, and for the next several hours she lay awake remembering the giddy, fun-filled hours she had spent with Michael. She could hardly wait for him to pick her up, and the excitement was keeping her as awake and alert as if she'd slept a week.

She was delighted with the way she looked. She and Kris had spent the afternoon experimenting with the tons of makeup the two of them had collected. She also finally broke down and let Kris put a henna rinse in her hair, and as Kris had promised, it had brought out the red highlights in her thick brown hair. Kris had also braided several strands of blue ribbon the color of the dress in Barbara's hair. With carefully made-up eyes, deep rose lipstick, and blush, Barbara looked almost exotic. Certainly she looked different from the girl she had been before her life had been touched by Michael.

From her jewelry box Barbara fished out a few rings and the silver locket her father had given her on her fifteenth birthday. It was then she noticed she had forgotten to do her nails.

She ran into the bathroom to get an emery board and began to file her fingernails. It'll have to do, she thought, realizing she had no nail polish. With Michael due any minute, she wouldn't have time to go out and get some. Unless . . .

"Mom," she called, running out into the hall. "Could you come up here?"

A few minutes later her mother dashed up the stairs, went into her room, and came out with a bottle of dusty pink nail gloss. "Need this?" she said, holding out the bottle to her daughter.

"Mom, how'd you know?"

"I'm not too old to remember my prom," she said. "Honey, you look so beautiful. Just wait till your father sees you."

"I'm glad he didn't put up a fuss about last night."

"Don't you know how proud he is of you? It almost broke his heart when he realized his little girl might not be going to her own prom. I think he's ready to shoot Michael for not asking you sooner."

"It's not his fault," Barbara said. "Anyway, you're going to like him, Mom. He's wonderful."

"To grab you he must be. Hurry up, your father wants to take a picture of you."

Holding her wet nails in front of her, Barbara carefully stepped down the stairs to the living room, sidestepping Macbeth, who yapped playfully around her.

"My little girl." Mr. Vreeland sighed.

"I'm not so little anymore," Barbara noted.

"I see . . . You just be sure this Michael behaves himself," he warned.

"Oh, Daddy," she scoffed. She was about to say more but was interrupted by the doorbell. "He's here!"

"I'll get it," her mother said, Macbeth running to the door behind her. "Come on in, Michael. I'm Mrs. Vreeland. Barbara's waiting for you over here."

Michael took two steps inside, then stopped at the sight of Barbara. She smiled shyly, then politely introduced him to her father. Michael said hello to him, but Barbara couldn't help but see that he couldn't take his eyes off her! Actually, she was having trouble keeping her eyes off him. Dressed in a white tuxedo with a light-blue shirt and tie, he looked as if he had stepped out of a picture in the fashion section of the L.A. *Times*.

"I got this for you." He handed her a florist's box. "I wasn't sure what color dress you had, so I got a white one."

"It's beautiful," Barbara said, taking the white rose corsage out of the box. She stood still as Michael pinned it on the left side of her dress.

"Over the heart," he noted.

"What a romantic," she sighed.

"Wait, you two," Mr. Vreeland said. "I want a picture before you go."

As Barbara's father went to get the camera, Michael whispered, "Seems I'm not the only sentimental one around here."

After Mr. Vreeland had taken several shots with his camera, Barbara and Michael walked down the flagstone path to his car. The night sky was glowing with a nearly full moon, and there was just enough of a nip in the air to make Barbara glad she had borrowed her mother's silk wrap.

"Like my chariot, Cinderella?"

"It's beautiful," Barbara said, admiring the cream colored BMW.

"It's my dad's," Michael said, opening up the door for her. "I didn't want to take the chance of you messing up your dress in my heap."

The short ride to the school didn't leave much time for small talk. Before long they had pulled up to the parking lot. Even from there they could hear the band tuning up for the evening's festivities.

With the lights dimmed low and little candles on each of the two dozen round tables, the gym had taken on a quiet, romantic look. Unaccustomed to the ambiance, Barbara had to squint to make out the couples already in the room. Before long she was able to spot Kris and Mark getting settled at a table next to the dance floor, and she led Michael over there. She wanted to share this night with the two people who meant the most to her.

Just as they arrived Barbara was approached by Joanne, who was wearing a daring, tawny-colored jumpsuit. Standing next to her was a beaming Benji, looking surprisingly good in a tan tuxedo and a new pair of aviator glasses.

"You mind if we put our things down here?" she asked Barbara. "We're going to dance."

"There's plenty of room," Barbara answered.

After the couple left, Barbara confided to Michael, "I forgot to tell you. I'm not a very good dancer."

"That's okay, neither am I."

"I seem to remember you were pretty good that day in the *Call*."

"You were lucky I didn't step all over your feet."

"If you're willing to make a fool out of yourself over there, so am I," she said. "You game?"

"Anything for my Felix."

To her delight Barbara discovered dancing to the band was more than easy. All she had to do was stay close to Michael and sway with him to the music.

"It's not so hard, after all, is it?" Michael whispered in her ear.

"Dancing? No," she answered.

"No, I meant being with me."

She looked up to him and smiled. "It's the easiest thing in the world."

In response, he lifted her up in the air a few inches and twirled her around in a big circle.

"Hey," she said as he lowered her gently. "I admit you've knocked me off my feet, but do you have to demonstrate it?"

"Again and again and again."

They danced, holding each other close as if they had both discovered something special and too precious to let go. Finally, when the band switched over to rock 'n' roll, the two of them decided to leave the floor to the real dancers and get back to their table.

The room was nearly full now, but they hardly noticed anyone but each other. Barbara still couldn't believe it had really happened, that she had made it to the prom with Michael. She had wasted so much time because of her fears, and she was determined to make up for it.

"It's so beautiful here," she said after a while. With the real palm trees and flowers and Kevin's very effective murals, she really felt as if she was at a beachside resort, one devoted to people in love. She took another look at Jo-anne's purse and wondered why she hadn't settled herself at the Sigma table on the other side of the dance floor. But a quick look answered the question: Brian and his new girl-friend Wendy were already seated there. But Joanne, still dancing happily with Benji, didn't seem too concerned with the snub from her old friends.

"Hope we're not interrupting," Kris said, coming off the dance floor with Mark. Having given up her search for a blue gown, she had ended up with a red strapless dress that looked great on her. From the way Mark was looking at her, he didn't seem disappointed at all.

"You looked pretty good out there," Barbara told her.

"Don't give me that," she kidded. "I know where your eyes were."

"Just trying to make conversation," Barbara said, red-faced, having been caught in a fib.

"I'll forgive you this time," Kris said.

Michael and Mark left the table to bring back drinks for the girls.

"Isn't he a doll?" Kris asked, watching them walk off.

"He sure is," Barbara said dreamily.

"He was worth the wait," Kris added.

"That's for sure."

"I mean Mark," Kris pointed out.

"Yeah, he's not bad, either," Barbara offered.

They both looked at each other and laughed, happy that things had worked out so well.

The next few hours were like a magical dream to Barbara. There were moments when she wondered if she would wake up and discover it was all the product of an overactive imagination. But then she would look at Michael and touch his hand and realize that the next day they would still be together.

At one point, as Barbara was coming off the dance floor with Michael, her eyes met Miss Gregg's for a second, and she saw the young teacher wink approvingly. She and Mr. Rozzo were two of the chaperons for the prom, and Barbara hoped they were having as good a time as she was.

Much sooner than she would have liked, it was time for the final dance of the evening. Michael and Barbara got up from their seats, walking by Lisa and Scott, who had been designated king and queen of the prom. They had been the sentimental favorite in the balloting. Soon after they had called off their engagement, they had realized that just being steadies was a much more enjoyable situation, and they began to walk around the Clear Lake halls like a couple of lovebirds. It was a happy ending for now, and with the whole class rooting for them, they'd won the royal honors hands down.

Soon after they began dancing, Barbara said to Michael, "I think I'll devote the entire front page of the *Call* to this prom."

"You call this news?"

"Don't you think so?"

"Well, if that's the case, I have a suggestion

for a sidebar. Two columns under the headline: Barbara and Michael fall in love."

She moved closer to him.

"Now let's pose for the picture," he said. Right there in the middle of the floor, Michael tenderly kissed his new girlfriend.

Barbara's sweet dream had become a reality.